THE FRENCH TWINS by Lucy Fitch Perkins

Lucy Fitch Perkins was forty-eight when she was approached by a publisher friend who, impressed by her talents as both an illustrator and writer, which he knew through correspondence, urged her to write. He was so earnest that she thought of an idea for a children's book the next morning, and she immediately set to work making sketches and preparing the idea for presentation. The publisher came to dinner at their house the next evening and she showed him the idea. His response was immediate "go ahead and write it, and I want it". That book was The Dutch Twins, the first in what became a long running and wildly popular series. Here we publish another in that series 'The French Twins'.

Index Of Contents

CHAPTER I. THE CHURCH AND THE PEOPLE

The sunlight of the clear September afternoon shone across the roofs of the City of Rheims, and fell in a yellow flood upon the towers of the most beautiful cathedral in the world, turning them into two shining golden pillars against the deep blue of the eastern sky.

The streets below were already in shadow, but the sunshine still poured through the great rose window above the western portal, lighting the dim interior of the church with long shafts of brilliant reds, blues, and greens, and falling at last in a shower of broken color upon the steps of the high altar. Somewhere in the mysterious shadows an unseen musician touched the keys of the great organ, and the voice of the Cathedral throbbed through its echoing aisles in tremulous waves of sound. Above the deep tones of the bass notes a delicate melody floated, like a lark singing above the surf.

Though the great church seemed empty but for sound and color, there lingered among its shadows a few persons who loved it well. There were priests and a few worshipers. There was also Father Varennes, the Verger, and far away in one of the small chapels opening from the apse in the eastern end good Mother Meraut was down upon her knees, not praying as you might suppose, but scrubbing the stone floor. Mother Meraut was a wise woman; she knew when to pray and when to scrub, and upon occasion did both with equal energy to the glory of God and the service of his Church. Today it was her task to make the little chapel clean and sweet, for was not the Abbe coming to examine the Confirmation Class in its catechism, and were not her own two children, Pierre and Pierette, in the class? In time to the heart-beats of the organ, Mother Meraut swept her brush back and forth, and it was already near the hour for the class to assemble when at last she set aside her scrubbing-pail, wiped her hands upon her apron, and began to dust the chairs which had been standing outside the arched entrance, and to place them in orderly rows within the chapel.

She had nearly completed her task, when there was a tap-tapping upon the stone floor, and down the long aisle, leaning upon his crutch, came Father Varennes. He stopped near the chapel and watched her as she whisked the last chair into place and then paused with her hands upon her hips to make a final inspection of her work.

"Bonjour, Antoinette," said the Verger.

Mother Meraut turned her round, cheerful face toward him. "Ah, it is you, Henri," she cried, "come, no doubt, to see if the chapel is clean enough for the Abbe! Well, behold."

The Verger peered through the arched opening, and sniffed the wet, soapy smell which pervaded the air. "One might even eat from your clean floor, Antoinette," he said, smiling, "and taste nothing worse with his food than a bit of soap. Truly the chapel is as clean as a shriven soul."

"It's a bold bit of dirt that would try to stand out against me," declared Mother Meraut, with a flourish of her dust-cloth, "for when I go after it I think to myself, 'Ah, if I but had one of those detestable Germans by the nose, how I would grind it!' and the very thought brings such power to my elbow that I check myself lest I wear through the stones of the floor."

The Verger laughed, then shook his head. "Truly, Antoinette," he said, "I believe you could seize your husband's gun if he were to fall, and fill his place in the Army as well as you fill his place here in the Cathedral, doing a man's work with a woman's strength, and smiling as if it were but play! Our France can never despair while there are women like you."

"My Jacques shall carry his own gun," said Mother Meraut, stoutly, "and bring it home with him when the war is over, if God wills, and may it be soon! Meanwhile I will help to keep our holy Cathedral clean as he used to do. It is not easy work, but one must do what one can, and surely it is better to do it with smiles than with tears!"

The Verger nodded. "That is true," he said, "yet it is hard to smile in the face of sorrow."

"But we must smile, though our hearts break, for France, and for our children, lest they forget joy!" cried Mother Meraut. She smiled as she spoke, though her lip trembled "I will you the truth, Henri, sometimes when I think of what the Germans have already done in Belgium, and may yet do in France, I feel my heart breaking in my bosom. And then I say to myself, 'Courage, Antoinette! It is our business to live bravely for the France that is to be when this madness is over. Our armies are still between us and the Boche. It is not time to be afraid.'"

"And I tell you, they shall not pass," cried Father Varennes, striking his crutch angrily upon the stone floor. "The brave soldiers of France will not permit it! Oh, if I could but carry a gun instead of this!" He rattled his crutch despairingly as he spoke.

Mother Meraut sighed. "Though I am a woman, I too wish I might fight the invaders," she said, "but since I may not carry a gun, I will put all the more energy into my broom and sweep the dirt from the Cathedral as I would sweep the Germans back to the Rhine if I could."

"It is, indeed, the only way for women, children, and such as I," grieved the Verger.

"Tut, tut," answered Mother Meraut cheerfully, "it isn't given us to choose our service. If God had wanted us to fight he would have given us power to do it."

The Verger shook his head. "I wish I were sure of that," he said, "for there's going to be need for all the fighting blood in France if half one hears is true. They say now that the Germans are already far over the French border and that our Army is retreating before them. The roads are more than ever crowded with refugees, and the word they bring is that the Germans have already reached the valley of the Aisne."

"But that is at our very doors!" cried Mother Meraut. "It is absurd, that rumor. Chicken hearts! They listen to nothing but their fears. As for me, I will not believe it until I must. I will trust in the Army as I do in my God and the holy Saints."

"Amen," responded the Verger devoutly.

At this moment the great western portal swung on its hinges, a patch of light showed itself against the gloom of the interior of the Cathedral, and the sound of footsteps and of fresh young voices mingled with the tones of the organ.

"It's the children, bless their innocent hearts," said Mother Meraut. "I hear the voices of my Pierre and Pierrette."

"And I of my Jean," said the Verger, starting hastily down the aisle. "The little magpies forget they must be quiet in the House of God!" He shook his finger at them and laid it warningly upon his lips. The noise instantly subsided, and it was a silent and demure little company that tiptoed up the aisle, bent the knee before the altar, and then filed past Mother Meraut into the chapel which she had made so clean.

Pierre and Pierrette led the procession, and Mother Meraut beamed with pride as they blew her a kiss in passing. They were children that any mother might be proud of. Pierrette had black, curling hair and blue eyes with long black lashes, and Pierre was a straight, tall, and manly-looking boy. The Twins were nine years old.

Mother Meraut knew many of the children in the Confirmation Class, for they were all schoolmates and companions of Pierre and Pierrette. There was Paul, the sore of the inn-keeper, with Marie, his sister. There was Victor, whose father rang the Cathedral chimes. There were David and Genevieve, and Madeleine and Virginie and Etienne, and last of all there was jean, the Verger's son, little Jean, the youngest in the class. Mother Meraut nodded to them all as they passed.

Promptly on the first stroke of the hour the Abbe appeared in the north transept of the Cathedral and made his way with quick, decided steps toward the chapel. He was a young man with thick dark hair almost concealed beneath his black three-cornered cap, and as he walked, his long black soutane swung about him in vigorous folds. When he appeared in the door of the chapel the class rose politely to greet him. "Bonjour, my children," said the Abbe, and then, turning his back upon them, bowed before the crucifix upon the chapel altar.

Mother Meraut and the Verger slipped quietly away to their work in other portions of the church, and the examination began. First the Abby asked the children to recite the Lord's Prayer, the Creed, and the Ten Commandments in unison, and when they had done this without a mistake, he said "Bravo! Now I wonder if you can each do as well alone? Let me see, I will call upon -" He paused and looked about as if he were searching for the child who was most likely to do it well.

Three girls; Genevieve, Virginie, and Pierrette, raised their hands and waved them frantically in the air, but, curiously enough, the Abbe did not seem to see them. Instead his glance fell upon Pierre, who was gazing thoughtfully at the vaulted ceiling and hoping with all his heart that the Abbe would not call upon him. "Pierre!" he said, and any one looking at him very closely might have seen a twinkle in his eye as Pierre withdrew his gaze from the ceiling and struggled reluctantly to his feet. "You may recite the Ten Commandments."

Pierre began quite glibly, "Thou shalt have no other gods before me," and went on, with only two mistakes and one long wait, until he had reached the fifth. "Thou shalt not kill," he recited, and then to save his life he could not think what came next. He gazed imploringly at the ceiling again, and at the high stained-glass window, but they told him nothing. He kicked backward gently, hoping that Pierrette, who sat next, would prompt him, but she too failed to respond. "I'll ask a question," thought Pierre desperately, "and while the Abbe is answering maybe it will come to me." Aloud he said: "If you please, your reverence, I don't understand about that commandment. It says, 'Thou shalt not kill,' and yet our soldiers have gone to war on purpose to kill Germans, and the priests blessed them as they marched away!"

This was indeed a question! The class gasped with astonishment at Pierre's boldness in asking it. The Abbe paused a moment before answering. Then he said, "If you, Pierre, were to shoot a man in the street in order to take his purse, would that be wrong?"

"Yes," answered the whole class.

"Very well," said the Abbe, "so it would. But if you should see a murderer attack your mother or your sister, and you should kill him before he could carry out his wicked purpose, would that be just the same thing?"

"No," wavered the class, a little doubtfully.

"If instead of defending your mother or sister you were simply to stand aside and let the murderer kill them both, you would really be helping the murderer, would you not? It is like that today in France. An enemy is upon us who seeks to kill us so that he may rob us of our beautiful home land. God sees our hearts. He knows that the soldiers of France go forth not to kill Germans but to save France! not wantonly to take life, but because it is the only way to save lives for which they themselves are ready to die. Ah, my children, it is one thing to kill as a murderer kills; it is quite another to be willing to die that others may live! Our Blessed Lord"

The Abbe lifted his hand to make the sign of the Cross but it was stayed in mid-air. The sentence he had begun was never finished, for at that moment the great bell in the Cathedral tower began to ring. It was not the clock striking the hour; it was not the chimes calling the people to prayer. Instead, it was the terrible sound of the alarm bell ringing out a warning to the people of Rheims that the Germans were at their doors.

Wide-eyed with terror, the children sprang from their seats, but the Abbe, with hand uplifted, blocked the entrance and commanded them to stay where they were.

"Let no one leave the Cathedral," he cried.

At this instant Mother Meraut appeared upon the threshold searching for her children, and behind her, coming as fast as his lameness would permit, came the Verger. The Abbe turned to them. "I leave these children all in your care," he said. "Stay with them until I return."

And without another word he disappeared in the shadows.

Mother Meraut sat down on one of the chairs she had dusted so carefully, and gathered the frightened children about her as a hen gathers her chickens under her wing. "There, now," she said cheerfully, as she wiped their tears upon the corner of her apron, "let's save our tears until we really know what we have to cry for. There never yet was misery that couldn't be made worse by crying, anyway. The boys will be brave, of course, whatever happens. And the girls, surely they will remember that it was a girl who once saved France, and meet misfortune bravely, like our blessed Saint Jeanne d'Arc."

The Cathedral organ had ceased to fill the great edifice with sweet and inspiring sounds. Instead, there now was only the muffled tread of marching feet, the rumble of heavy wheels, and the low, ominous beating of drums to break the stillness.

Mother Meraut and the children waited obediently in the chapel, scarcely breathing in their suspense, while Father Varennes went tap-tapping up and down the aisles eagerly watching for the Abbe to reappear. At last he came. Mother Meraut, the Verger, and the children all crowded about him, waiting breathlessly for him to speak.

The Abbe was pale, but his voice was firm. "I have been to the north tower," he said, "and there I could see for miles in every direction.
Far away to the east and north are massed the hordes of the German Army; they are coming toward Rheims as a thunder-cloud comes rolling over the sky. Between us and them is our Army, but alas, their faces are turned this way. They are retreating before the German hosts! Already French troops are marching through Rheims; already the streets are filled with people who are fleeing from their homes for fear of the Boche. Unless God sends a miracle, our City is indeed doomed, for a time at least, to wear the German yoke."

He paused, and the children burst into wild weeping. Mother Meraut hushed them with comforting words. "Do not cry, my darlings," she said. "God is not dead, and we shall yet live to see justice done and our dear land restored to us. The soldiers now in the streets are all our own brave defenders. We shall be able to go in safety, even though in sorrow, to our homes."

"Come," said the Abbe, "there is no time to lose. Our Army will, without doubt, make a stand on the plains west of the City, and it will not be long before the Germans pass through. You must go to your homes as fast as possible. Henri, you remain here with your Jean, that you may meet any of the parents who come for their children. Tell them I have gone with them myself and will deliver each child safely at his own door."

"I can take cart of my own," said Mother Meraut. "You need have no fear for us."

"Very well," said the Abbe, and, calling the rest of the children about him, he marched them down the aisle and out into the street.

Mother Meraut followed with Pierre and Pierrette. At the door they paused and stood for a moment under the great sculptured arches to survey the scene before them. The great square before the Cathedral was filled with people, some weeping, others standing about as if dazed by sorrow. Between the silent crowds which lined the sidewalks passed the soldiers, grim and with set faces, keeping time to the throbbing of the drums as they marched. Above the scene, in the center of the square, towered the beautiful statue of Jeanne d'Arc, mounted upon her charger and lifting her sword toward the sky.

"Ah," murmured Mother Meraut to herself, "our blessed Maid still keeps guard above the City!" She lifted her clasped hands toward the statue. "Blessed Saint Jeanne," she prayed, "hear us in Paradise, and come once more to save our beautiful France!"

Then, waving a farewell to the Verger and Jean, who had followed them to the door, she took her children by the hand and plunged with them into the sad and silent crowd.

CHAPTER II. ON THE WAY HOME

For some time after leaving the Cathedral, Mother Meraut and the Twins lingered in the streets, forgetful of everything but the retreating Army and the coming invasion. Everywhere there were crowds surging to and fro. Some were hastening to close their places of business and put up their shutters before the Germans should arrive. Some were hurrying through the streets carrying babies and bundles. Others were wheeling their few belongings upon barrows or in baby-carriages. Still others flew by on bicycles with packages of clothing fastened to the handle-bars; and there were many automobiles loaded to the brim with household goods and fleeing families.

Doors were flung open and left swinging on their hinges as people escaped, scarcely looking behind them as they fled. These were refugees from Rheims itself. There were many others wearily plodding through the City, people who had come from Belgium and the border towns of France. Some who had come from farms drove pitiful cattle before them, and some journeyed in farm wagons, with babies and old people, chickens, dogs, and household goods mixed in a heap upon beds of straw. In all the City there was not a cheerful sight, and everywhere, above all other sounds, were heard the rumble of wheels, the sharp clap-clap of horses' hoofs upon the pavement, and the steady beat of marching feet.

At last, weary and heartsick, the three wanderers turned into a side street and stepped into a little shop where food was sold. "We must have some supper," said Mother Meraut to the Twins, "Germans or no Germans! One cannot carry a stout heart above an empty stomach! And if it is to be our last meal in French Rheims, let us at least make it a good one!" Though there was a catch in her voice, she smiled almost gaily as she spoke. "Who knows?" she went on. "Perhaps after to-morrow we shall be able to get nothing but sauerkraut and sausage!"

The shop was not far from the little home of the Merauts, and they often bought things of stout Madame Coudert, whose round face with its round spectacles rose above the counter like a full moon from behind a cloud. "Ah, mon amie," said Mother Meraut as she entered the shop, "it is good to see you sitting in your place and not running away like a hare before the hounds!"

Madame Coudert shrugged her shoulders. "But of what use is it to run when one has no place to run to?" she demanded. "As for me, I stay by the shop and die at least respectably among my own cakes and pies. To run through the country and die at last in a ditch, it would not suit me at all!"

"Bravo," cried Mother Meraut triumphantly. "Just my own idea! My children and I will remain in our home and take what comes, rather than leap from the frying-pan into the fire as so many are doing. If every one runs away, there will be no

Rheims at all." Then to Pierre and Pierrette she said "Choose, each of you. What shall we buy for our supper?"

Pierre pointed a grimy finger at a small cake with pink frosting. "That," he said briefly.

His mother smiled. "Ah, Pierre, that sweet-tooth of yours!" she cried. "Like Marie Antoinette you think if one lacks bread one may eat cakes! And now it is Pierrette's turn; only be quick, ma mie, for it is already late."

"Eggs," said Pierrette promptly, "for one of your savory omelets, mamma, and a bit of cheese."

The purchases were quickly made, and, having said good-night to Madame Coudert, they hurried on to the little house in the Rue Charly where they lived. When they reached home, it was already quite dark. Mother Meraut hastened up the steps and unlocked the door, and in less time than it takes to tell it her bonnet was off, the fire was burning, and the omelet was cooking on the stove.

Pierrette set the table. "I'm going to place father's chair too," she said to her mother. "He is no doubt thinking of us as we are of him, and it will make him stem nearer."

Mother Meraut nodded her head without speaking, and wiped her eyes on her apron as she slid the omelet on to a hot plate. Then she seated herself opposite the empty chair and with a steady voice prayed for a blessing upon the food and upon the Armies of France.

When they had finished supper, cleared it away, and put the kitchen in order, Mother Meraut pointed to the clock. "Voila!" she cried, "hours past your bedtime, and here you are still flapping about like two young owls! To bed with you as fast as you can go."

"But, Mother," began Pierre.

"Not a single 'but,'" answered his Mother, wagging her finger at him. "Va!"

The children knew protest was useless, and in a few minutes they were snugly tucked away. Long after they were both sound asleep, their Mother sat with her head bowed upon the table, listening, listening to the distant sound of marching feet. At last, worn out with grief and anxiety, she too undressed, said her rosary, and, after a long look at her sleeping children, blew out the candle and crept into bed beside Pierrette.

Silence and darkness settled down upon the little household, and, for a time at least, their sorrows were forgotten in the blessed oblivion of sleep.

CHAPTER III. THE COMING OF THE GERMANS

When the Twins opened their eyes the next morning, the first thing they saw was the sun shining in at the eastern window of the kitchen, and Mother Meraut bending over the fire. There was a smell of chocolate in the air, and on the table there were rolls and butter. Pierre yawned and rubbed his eyes. Pierrette sat up and tried to think what it was she was so unhappy about; sleep had, for the time being, swept the terrors of the night quite out of her mind. In an instant more the fearful truth rolled over her like a wave, and she sank back upon the pillow with a little moan.

Her Mother heard and understood. She too had waked from sleep to sorrow, but she only cried out cheerfully, "Bonjour, my sleepy heads! Last night you did not want to go to your beds at all. This morning you wish not to leave them! Hop into your clothes as fast as you can, or we shall be late."

"Late where?" asked Pierre.

"To my work at the Cathedral, to be sure," answered Mother Meraut promptly. "Where else? Did you think the Germans would make me sit at home and cry for terror while my work waits? Whoever rules in Rheims, the Cathedral still stands and must be kept clean."

It was wonderful how the dismal world brightened to Pierre and Pierrette as they heard their Mother's brave voice. They flew out of bed at once and were dressed in a twinkling.

While they ate their breakfast, Pierre thought of a plan. "We ought to take a lot of food with us to-day," he said to his Mother. "There's no telling what may happen before night. Maybe we can't get home at all and shall have to sleep in the Cathedral."

"Oh," shuddered Pierrette, "among all those tombs?"

"There are worse places where one might sleep," said the Mother. "The dead are less to be feared than the living, and the Cathedral is the safest place in Rheims." She brought out a wicker basket and began to pack it with food as she talked. First she put in two pots of jam. "There," said she, "that's the jam Grandmother made from her gooseberries at the farm."

She paused, struck by a new alarm. Her father and mother lived in a tiny village far west of Rheims. What if the Germans should succeed in getting so far as that? What would become of them? She shut her fears in her breast, saying nothing to the children, and went on filling the basket. "Here is a bit of cheese left from last night. I'll put that in, and a pat of butter," she said; "but we must stop at Madame Coudert's for more bread. You two little pigs have eaten every scrap there was in the house."

"There are eggs left," suggested Pierrette.

"So there are, ma mie," said her Mother. "We will boil them all and take them with us. There's a great deal of nourishment in eggs." She flew to get the saucepan, and while the eggs bubbled and boiled on the stove, she and the children set the little kitchen in order and got themselves ready for the street.

It was after nine o'clock when at last Mother Meraut took the basket on her arm and gave Pierrette her knitting to carry, and the three started down the steps.

"Everything looks just the same as it did yesterday," said Pierrette as they walked down the street. "There's that little raveled-out dog that always barks at Pierre, and there's Madame Coudert's cat asleep on the railing, just as she always is."

"Yes," said Mother Meraut, with a sigh, "the cats and dogs are the same, it is only the people who are different!"

They entered the shop and exchanged greetings with Madame Coudert. They had bought a long loaf of bread, and Mother Meraut was just opening her purse to pay for it, when suddenly a shot rang out. It was followed by the rattle of falling tiles. Another and another came, and soon there was a perfect rain of shot and shell.

"It is the Germans knocking at the door of Rheims before they enter," remarked Madame Coudert with grim humor. "I did not expect so much politeness!"

Mother Meraut did not reply. For once her cheerful tongue found nothing comforting to say. Pierre clung to her arm, and Pierrette put her fingers in her ears and hid her face against her Mother's breast.

For some time the deafening sounds continued. From the window they could see people running for shelter in every direction. A man came dashing down the street; dodging falling tiles as he ran, and burst into Madame Coudert's shop. He had just come from the Rue Colbert and had news to tell. "The Boches have sent an emissary to the Mayor to demand huge supplies of provisions from the City, and a great sum of money besides," he told them, as he gasped for breath. "They are shelling the champagne cellars and the public buildings of the City to scare us into giving them what they demand. The German Army will soon be here."

In a few moments there was a lull in the roar of the guns, and then in the distance another sound was heard. It was a mighty song of triumph as the conquerors came marching into Rheims!

"There won't be any more shooting for a while anyway," said the stranger, who had now recovered his breath. "They won't shell the City while it's full of their own men. I'm going to see them come in."

All Pierre's fears vanished in an instant. "Come on," he cried, wild with excitement; "let us go too."

"I'll not stir a foot from my shop," said Madame Coudert firmly. "I don't want to see the Germans, and if they want to see me, they can come where I am."

But Pierre had not waited for a reply, from her or any one else. He was already running up the street.

"Catch him, catch him," gasped Mother Meraut.

Pierrette dashed after Pierre, and as she could run like the wind, she soon caught up with him and seized him by the skirt of his blouse. "Stop! stop!" she screamed. "Mother doesn't want you to go."

But she might as well have tried to argue with a hurricane. Pierre danced up and down with rage, as Pierrette braced herself, and firmly anchored him by his blouse. "Leggo, leggo!" he shrieked. "I'm going, I tell you! I'm not afraid of any Germans alive."

Just then, panting and breathless, Mother Meraut arrived upon the scene. While Pierrette held on to his blouse, she attached herself to his left ear. It had a very calming effect upon Pierre. He stopped tugging to get away lest he lose his ear.

"Foolish boy," said his Mother, "see how much trouble you give me! You shall see the Germans, but you shall not run away from me. If we should get separated, God only knows whether we should ever find each other again."

The music had grown louder and louder, and was now very near. "I'll stay with you, if you'll only go," pleaded Pierre, "but you aren't even moving."

"Come, Pierrette," said his Mother, "take hold of his left arm. I will attend to his right; he might forget again. What he really needs is a bit and bridle!"

The three moved up the street, Pierre chafing inwardly, but helpless in his Mother's grasp, and at the next crossing the great spectacle burst upon them. A whole regiment of cavalry was passing, singing at the top of their lungs, "Lieb' Vaterland, macht ruhig sein." The sun glistened on their helmets, and the clanking of swords and the jingling of spurs kept time with the swelling chorus. After the cavalry came soldiers on foot, miles of them.

"Oh," murmured Pierrette, clinging to her Mother, "it's like a river of men!"

Her Mother did not answer. Pierrette looked up into her face. The tears were streaming down her cheeks, but her head was proudly erect. She looked at the other French people about them. There were tears on many cheeks, but not a head was bowed. Pierre was glaring at the troops and muttering through his teeth: "Just you wait till I grow up! I'll make you pay for this, you pirates! I'll -"

"Hush!" whispered Pierrette. "Suppose they should hear you!"

"I don't care if they do! I wish they would!" raged Pierre. "I'm going -"

But the German Army was destined not to suffer the consequences of Pierre's wrath. He did not even have a chance to tell Pierrette his plan for their destruction, for at this point his Mother, unable longer to endure the sight, dragged him forcibly from the scene. "They shall not parade their colors before me," she said firmly, "I will not stand still and look in silence upon my conquerors! If I could but face them with a gun, that would be different!"

She led the children through a maze of small streets by a roundabout way to the Cathedral, and there they were met at the entrance by the Verger, who gazed at them with sad surprise. "You've been out in the street during the bombardment," he said reproachfully. "It's just like you, Antoinette."

"Oh, but how was I to know it was coming?" cried Mother Meraut. "We left home before it began!"

"It would have been just the same if you had known," scolded the Verger. "Germans or devils, it would make no difference to you! You have no fear in you."

"You misjudge me," cried Mother Meraut; "but what good would it do to sit and quake in my own house? There is no safety anywhere, and here at least there is work to do."

"You can go about your work as usual with the noise of guns ringing in your ears and the Germans marching through Rheims?" exclaimed the Verger.

"Why not?" answered Mother Meraut, with spirit. "I guess our soldiers don't knock off work every time a gun goes off or a few Germans come in sight! It would be a shame if we could not follow their example!"

"Antoinette, you are a wonderful woman. I have always said so," declared the Verger solemnly. "You are as brave as a man!"

"Pooh!" said Mother Meraut, mockingly. "As if the men, bless their hearts, were so much braver than women, anyway! Oh, la! la! the conceit of you!" She wagged a derisive finger at the Verger, and, calling the children, went to get her scrubbing-pail and brushes.

All day long, while distant guns roared, she went about her daily tasks, keeping one spot of order and cleanliness in the midst of the confusion, disorder, and destruction of the invaded city. The Twins were busy, too; their Mother saw to that. They dusted chairs and placed them in rows; and at noon they found a corner where the light falling through one of the beautiful stained-glass windows made a spot of cheerful color in the gloom, and there they ate part of the lunch which they had packed in the wicker basket. During all the excitement of the morning they had not forgotten the lunch!

When the day's work was done, they ventured out upon the streets in the gathering dusk. They found them full of German soldiers, drinking, swaggering, singing, and they saw many strange and terrifying sights in the havoc wrought by the first bombardment. As they passed the door of Madame Coudert's shop, they peeped in and saw her sitting stolidly behind the counter, knitting.

"Oh," said Pierrette, "doesn't it seem like a year since we were here this morning?"

Mother Meraut called out a cheerful greeting to Madame Coudert. "Still in your place, I see," she said.

"Like the Pyramids," came the calm answer; and, cheered by her fortitude, they hurried on their way to the little house in the Rue Charly.

Mother Meraut sighed with relief as she unlocked the door. "Everything just as we left it," she said. "We at least shall have one more night in our own home." Then she drew the children into the shelter of the dear, familiar roof and locked the door from the inside.

CHAPTER IV. THE RETURN OF THE FRENCH

One unhappy day followed upon another for the inhabitants of Rheims. Each night they went to bed in terror; each morning they rose to face new trials and dangers. Yet their spirit did not fail. Each day the roar of guns toward the west grew fainter and more distant, and the people knew with sinking hearts that the Germans had driven the Armies of France farther and farther back toward Paris. Each day the conduct of the conquerors grew more arrogant. "Our Emperor will soon be in Paris!" they said.

On the public monuments and in the squares of the City appeared German proclamations printed upon green paper, warning the people of Rheims of terrible punishments which would befall them if they in any way rebelled against the will of the victorious invaders. It was only with great difficulty that Pierre could be dragged by these signs. Each morning as they went to the Cathedral they had to pass several of them, and Pierrette and her Mother soon learned to take precautions against an outburst of rage which might bring down upon his rash head the wrath of the enemy. The eye of the Germans seemed everywhere. One of these posters was fixed to the window of Madame Coudert's shop. On the morning that it first appeared, Pierre in passing made a dash for the gutter, picked up a handful of mud, and threw it squarely into the middle of the poster.

Madame Coudert saw him, and winked solemnly, but did not move. His Mother instantly collared Pierre, and led him up a side street just in time to escape the clutches of a German officer who had seen him a block away, and came on the run after him. When, puffing and blowing, he at last reached the shop there was no one in sight except Madame Coudert behind her counter. The enraged officer pointed out the insult that had been offered his country.

Madame Coudert looked surprised and concerned. She followed the officer to the door, and gazed at the disfigured poster. "I will clean it at once," she said obligingly. She got out soap and a brush immediately, and when she had finished, her work had been so thoroughly done that not a spot of mud was left, but unfortunately the center of the poster was rubbed through and quite illegible, and the rest of it was all streaked and stained! "Will that do?" she asked the officer, looking at him with round, innocent eyes and so evident a desire to please that, in spite of an uneasy suspicion, he merely grunted and went his way.

The first time they came into the shop after this episode Madame Coudert gave Pierre a cake with pink frosting on it.

In this way a whole week dragged itself by, and, on the morning of the eighth day after the German entry into Rheims, Mother Meraut and the Twins left home earlier than usual in order to reach the Cathedral before the bombardment, which they had learned daily to expect, should begin. They found Madame Coudert in front of her shop; washing the window. A large corner of the poster was now gone. "It rained last night," she said to Mother Meraut, "and the green color ran down on my window. I had to wash it, and accidentally I rubbed off a corner of the poster. It can't be very good paper." She looked solemnly at Pierre. "Too bad, isn't it?" she said, and closed one eye behind her round spectacles.

"The weather seems to have damaged a good many of them, I notice," answered Mother Meraut, with just a suspicion of a smile. "The weather has been quite pleasant too, strange!"

"Weather - nothing!" said Pierre, scornfully. "I'll bet you that -"

It seemed as if Pierre was always being interrupted at just the most exciting moment of his remarks, but this time he interrupted himself. "What's that?" he said, stopping short. Madame Coudert, his Mother, and Pierrette, all stood perfectly still, their eyes wide, their lips parted, listening, listening! They heard cannon-shots, then music, toward the west, coming nearer, nearer.

"It is, oh, it is the Marseillaise!" shrieked Pierrette.

Mother Meraut and the Twins ran toward the sound. Now shouts were heard, joyous shouts, from French throats! Never had they heard such a sound! People came tumbling out of their houses, some not fully dressed but who cared? The French were returning victorious from the battle of the Marne. They were coming again into Rheims, driving the Germans before them! Ah, but when the red trousers actually appeared in the streets the populace went mad with joy! They embraced the soldiers; they marched beside them with tears streaming down their cheeks, singing "March on! March on!" as though they would split their throats. Pierre and Pierrette marched and sang with the others, their Mother close beside them.

On and on came the singing, joy-maddened people, right past Madame Coudert's shop, and there, standing on the curb, with a tray in her arms piled high with goodies, was Madame Coudert herself. The green poster was already torn in shreds and lying in the gutter. It even looked as if some one had stamped on it, and above her door waved the tricolor of France! "Come here," she cried to Pierre and Pierrette, "Quick! Hand these out to the soldiers as long as there's one left!"

Pierre seized a pink frosted cake, and ran with it to a Captain. Pierrette gave a sugar roll to the first soldier she could reach; other hands helped. Mother Meraut ran into the shop and brought out more cakes. Shop-keepers all along the way followed Madame Coudert's example, and soon people everywhere were bringing offerings of candy, chocolate, and cigars to the soldiers, and the streets suddenly blossomed with blue, white, and red flags. At the corner, near Madame Coudert's shop, Pierre had the joy of seeing the German officer who had tried to catch him surrender to the Captain who had taken the pink cake. Oh, what a moment that was for Pierre! He sprang into the gutter as the German passed and savagely jumped up and down upon the fragments of the green poster! It was a matter for bitter regret to him long after that the German did not seem to notice him.

The whole morning passed in such joy and excitement that it was nearly noon when at last Mother Meraut, beaming with happiness, and accompanied by a radiant Pierre and Pierrette, entered the Cathedral. They were astonished to find it no longer the silent and dim sanctuary to which they were accustomed. The Abbe' was there, and the Verger, looking quite distracted, was directing a group of men in moving the praying-chairs from the western end of the Cathedral, and the space where they had been was already covered with heaps of straw. Under the great choir at the western end there were piles of broken glass. Part of the wonderful rose window had been shattered by a shell, and lay in a million fragments on the stone floor.

Mother Meraut clasped her hands in dismay. "What does it all mean?" she demanded of the Verger, as he went tap-tapping by after the workmen. "What do you wish me to do?"

"Gather up every fragment of glass," said the Verger briefly, "and put them in a safe place. The wounded are on the way, and are to be housed in the Cathedral. We must be ready for them. There is no time to lose."

As Mother Meraut flew to carry out his directions, the Abbe' beckoned to the children. "Can you be trusted to do an errand for me?" he said.

"Yes, Your Reverence," answered Pierre.

"Very well," said the Abbe. "I want you to get for the towers two Red Cross flags. They must be the largest size, and we must have them soon. The wounded may arrive at any moment now, and the Red Cross will protect the Cathedral from shell-fire, for not even Germans would destroy a hospital." He gave them careful directions, and a note for the shop-keeper. "Now run along, both of you," he said. "Tell your Mother where you are going, and that I sent you."

In two minutes the Twins were on their way, but it was more than an hour before they got back. First, the shop-keeper was out, and when he got back it took him some time to find large enough flags. At last, however, they returned, each carrying one done up in a paper parcel.

"Here are the flags," Pierre announced proudly to the Verger, who met them at the entrance.

"Yes," said Father Varennes, "here they are, and here you are. Come in, your Mother wants to see you." The children followed him through the door, and although they had been told that the wounded were to be brought to the Cathedral, they were not prepared for the sight that met their eyes as they entered. On the heaps of straw lay tossing moaning men, in the gray uniforms of the German army.

Pierrette seized Pierre's hand. "Oh," she shuddered, "I didn't think they'd be Germans!"

"They aren't, all of them," said the Verger, a little huskily. "Some of them are French. The Church shelters them all."

Doctors in white aprons were already in attendance upon the wounded, and nurses with red crosses on the sleeves of their white uniforms flitted silently back and forth on errands of mercy. The two children, clinging to each other and gazing fearfully about them, followed the Verger down the aisle. As they passed a heap of straw upon which a wounded German lay, something bright rolled from it to them and dropped at Pierrette's feet. Pierre sprang to pick it up. It was a German helmet. Across the front of it were letters. Pierre spelled them "Gott mit uns." "What does that mean?" he asked the Verger.

"God with us," snorted Father Varennes. "I suppose the poor wretches actually believe He is."

The Abbe' was waiting for them in the aisle, and he took from them the flags and the helmet. He had heard the Verger's reply, and guessed what the question must have been. "My boy," he said, laying his hand gently upon Pierre's head for an instant, "God is not far from any of his children. It is they who, through sin, separate themselves from Him! But never mind theology now. Your Mother is waiting for you. I will take you to her."

The Twins thought it strange that the Abbe' should himself guide them to their Mother. They followed his broad back and swinging black soutane to the farthest corner of the hospital space. There, beside a mound of straw upon which was stretched a wounded soldier in French uniform, knelt their Mother, and the Twins, looking down, met the eyes of their own Father gazing up at them.

"Gently! my dears, gently!" cautioned their Mother, as the children fell upon their knees beside her in an agony of tears. "Don't cry! He is wounded, to be sure, but he will get well, though he can never again fight for France. We shall see him every day, and by and by he will be at home again with us."

Too stunned for speech, the Twins only kissed the blood-stained hands, and then their Mother led them away. Under the western arches she kissed them good-by. "Go now to Madame Coudert," she said, "and tell her your Father is here, and that I shall stay in the Cathedral. Ask her to take care of you for the night. In the morning, if it is quiet, come again to me."

Dazed, happy, grieved, the children obeyed. They found Madame Coudert beaming above her empty counter. "Bless you," she cried, when they gave her their Mother's message, "of course you can stay! There are no pink cakes for Pierre, but who cares for cakes now that the French are once more in Rheims! And to think you have your Father back again! Surely this is a happy day for you, even though he came back with a wound!"

CHAPTER V. AT MADAME COUDERT'S

The joy of the people of Rheims was short-lived. The Germans had been driven out, it is true, but they had gone only a short distance to the east, and there, upon the banks of the Aisne, had securely entrenched themselves, venting their rage upon the City by daily bombardments. From ten until two nearly every day the inhabitants of the stricken City for the most part sat in their cellars listening to the whistling of shells and the crash of falling timbers and tiles. When the noise ceased, they returned to the light and air once more and looked about to see the extent of the damage done. Dur ing the rest of the day they went about their routine as usual, hoping against hope that the French Armies, which were now between Rheims and the enemy, would be able not only to defend the City but to drive the Germans still farther toward the Rhine.

When the Twins reached the Cathedral the morning after the return of the French troops, they found their Father resting after an operation which had removed from his leg a piece of shell, which had nearly cost his life and would make him permanently lame. Their Mother met them as they came in. She was pale but smiling. "What a joy to see you!" she cried, as she pressed them to her breast. "You may take one look at your Father and throw him a kiss; then you must go back to Madame Coudert."

"Mayn't we stay with you and help take care of Father?" begged Pierre.

"No," answered his Mother firmly, "the sights here are not for young eyes. I can wait upon the nurses and keep things clean: My place is here for the present, but tomorrow, if all goes well, we will sleep once more in our own little home, if it is still standing. In the mean time, be good children, and mind Madame Coudert. Now run along before the shells begin to fall."

The Twins obediently trotted away, and regained the little shop just as the clock struck ten. The day seemed long to them, for their thoughts were with their parents, but Madame Coudert was so cheerful herself; and kept them so busy they had no time to mope. Pierrette helped make the little cakes, and Pierre scraped the remains of the icing from the mixing-bowl and ate it lest any be wasted. In some ways Pierre was a very thrifty boy. Then, too, Madame Coudert allowed them to stand behind the counter and help wait upon the customers. Moreover, there was Fifine, the cat, for Pierrette to play with, and the little raveled-out dog lived only two doors below; so they did not lack for entertainment.

The next evening their Mother called for them, as she had promised to do, and they once more had supper and slept beneath their own roof. For three days they followed this routine, going with their Mother to Madame Coudert's, where they spent the day, returning at night. On the fourth day they were again allowed to visit the Cathedral and to see their Father. "It will do him good to be with his children," the doctor had said, and so, while Mother Meraut attended to her duties, Pierre and Pierrette sat on each side of the straw bed where he lay, proud and responsible to be left in charge of the patient.

Pierre was bursting with curiosity to know about the Battle of the Marne. Not another boy of his acquaintance had a wounded father, and though his opportunities for seeing his friends had been few, he had already done a good deal of boasting; and was pointed out by other boys on the street as a person of special distinction. "Tell me about the battle, Father," he begged.

His Father lifted his tired eyes to a statue of Jeanne d'Arc, which was in plain sight from where he lay. "Well, my boy," he said after a pause, "there is much I should not wish you to know, but this I will tell you. On the day the battle turned, the watchword of the Army was Jeanne d'Arc. Our soldiers sprang to the attack with her name upon their lips, and some have sworn to me that they saw her ride before us into battle on her white charger, carrying in her hand the very banner which you see there upon the altar. I do not know whether or not it is true, but certainly the victory was with us, and I for my part find it easy to believe that our blessed Saint Jeanne has not forgotten France." He raised himself a little on his elbow and pointed to a place not far distant in the nave. "There," he said, "is the very spot upon which she knelt while her king was being crowned here in our Cathedral after she had driven our enemies from French soil and had given him his throne! The happiest moments of her life were here! What place should be revisited by her pure spirit if not Rheims? My children, I wish you every day to pray that she may come again to deliver France!" Exhausted by emotion and by the effort he had made, he sank back upon the straw and closed his eyes.

Pierrette took his hand. "Dear papa," she said, "every day we will pray to her as you say, and give thanks to the Bon Dieu that your life has been spared to us. If only your poor leg -" she stopped, overcome by tears.

Her Father opened his eyes and smiled. "Ah, little one, what is a leg more or less; or a life either for that matter, when our France is in danger?" he said. "Is it not so, Pierre?"

Pierre gulped. "France can have all of my legs!" he cried, in a burst of patriotism. "And when I'm big enough, I'm going to dig a hole in the ground and put in millions of tons of dynamite and blow up the whole of Germany! That's what I'm going to do!"

His Father's eyes twinkled. "It seems a long while to wait," he said, "because now you are only nine, you see."

Just then their Mother came toward the little group. "Magpies!" she cried, "it seems that you are talking my patient to death. Run along now to Madame Coudert." At the Cathedral entrance she kissed them, and then stood for a moment to watch them as they hurried down the street out of sight.

CHAPTER VI. THE BURNING OF THE CATHEDRAL

On the evening of the 18th of September, Mother Meraut was late in leaving the Cathedral, and it was nearly dark when she reached Madame Coudert's door. Pierrette sat on the steps waiting for her, with Fifine, the cat, in her arms. Madame Coudert was knitting, as usual, and Pierre was trying to teach the little raveled-out dog to stand on his hind legs. As their Mother appeared, the children sprang to meet her.

"How is Father?" cried Pierrette. It was always the first question when they saw her.

"Better," answered her Mother. "In another week or two the doctor thinks he can be moved."

She was about to enter the shop to speak to Madame Coudert, when the air was suddenly rent by a fearful roar of sound. She clasped her children in her arms. "It's like thunder," she said, patting them soothingly; "if you hear the roar you know at once that you aren't killed. Come, we must hurry to the cellar." But before she could take a single step in that direction there was another terrible explosion.

"Look, oh look!" screamed Pierre, pointing to the Cathedral towers, which were visible from where they stood; "they are shelling the Cathedral!"

For an instant they stood as if rooted to the spot. Was it possible the Germans would shell the place where their own wounded lay, a place protected by the cross? They saw the scaffolding about one of the towers burst suddenly into flames. In another moment the fire had caught and devoured the Red Cross flag itself and then sprang like a thing possessed to the roof. An instant more, and that too was burning.

"Father!" screamed Pierre, and before any one could stop him or even say a word, the boy was far up the street, running like a deer toward the Cathedral. Pierrette was but a few steps behind him.

When she saw her children rushing madly into such danger, Mother Meraut's exhausted body gave way beneath the demands of her spirit. If Madame Coudert had not caught her, she would have sunk down upon the step. It was only for an instant, but in that instant the children had passed out of sight. Not stopping even to close her door, Madame Coudert seized Mother Meraut's hand, and together the two women ran after them. But they could not hope to rival the speed of fleet young feet, and when they reached the Cathedral square the flames were already roaring upward into the very sky. The streets were crowded by this time, and their best speed brought them to the square ten minutes after the children had reached the burning Cathedral, and, heedless of danger, had dashed in and to the corner where their helpless Father lay.

The place was swarming with doctors and nurses working frantically to move the wounded. The Abbe' was there, and the Archbishop also. Already the straw had caught fire in several places from falling brands. "Out through the north transept," shouted the Abbe.

Pierre and Pierrette knew well what they had come to do. For them there was but one person in the Cathedral, and that person was their Father. They had but one purpose, to get him out. Young as they were, they were already well used to danger, and it scarcely occurred to them that they were risking their lives. Certainly they were not afraid. When they reached their Father's side, they found him vainly struggling to rise.

"Here we are, Father," shouted Pierre: "Lean on us!" He flew to one side; Pierrette was already struggling to lift him on the other. As his bed was the one farthest from the spot where the fire first appeared, the doctors and nurses had sought to rescue those in greatest danger, and so the children for the time being were alone in their effort to save him.

The flames were now leaping through the Cathedral aisles, devouring the straw beds as if they were tinder. In vain Father Meraut ordered them to leave him. For once his children refused to obey. Somehow they got him to his feet, and he, for their sakes making a superhuman effort, succeeded in staggering between them, using their lithe young bodies as crutches. How they reached the door of the north transept they never knew, but reach it they did, before the burning flames. And there a new terror appeared.

The people of Rheims, infuriated by the long abuse which they had suffered, stood with guns pointed at the wounded and helpless Germans whom the doctors and nurses had succeeded in getting so far on the way to safety. Above the roar of flames rose the roar of angry voices. "It is the Germans who burn our Cathedral. Let them die with it," shouted one.

Between the helpless Germans and the angry mob; facing their guns, towered the figures of the Abby and the Archbishop! "If you kill them, you must first kill us," cried the Archbishop. Kill the Archbishop and the Abbe'! Unthinkable! The guns were immediately lowered, and the work of rescue went on.

Out of the north door crept Father Meraut, supported by his brave children. "Bravo! Bravo!" shouted the crowd, and then hands that would have killed Germans willingly, were stretched in instant sympathy and helpfulness to the wounded French soldier and his brave children. Two men made a chair of their arms, and Father Meraut was carried in safety to the square before the Cathedral, Pierre and Pierrette following close behind. At the foot of the statue of Jeanne d'Arc they stopped to rest and change hands, and there, frantic with joy, Mother Meraut found them.

"A soldier of France, wounded at the Marne!" shouted the crowd, and if he had been able to endure it, they would have borne him upon their grateful shoulders. As it was, he was carried in no less grateful arms clear to Madame Coudert's door, and there, lying upon an improvised stretcher, and attended by his wife and children, he rested from his journey, while Madame Coudert ran to prepare a cup of coffee for a stimulant. From Madame Coudert's door they watched the further destruction of the beautiful Cathedral which Mother Meraut had so often called the "safest place in Rheims." As it burned, a wonderful thing happened. High above the glowing roof there suddenly flamed the blue fleur-de-lis of France!

"See! See!" cried Mother Meraut. "A Miracle! The Lily of France! Oh, surely it is a sign sent by the Bon Dieu to keep us from despair!"

"It is only the gas from an exploding shell, bursting in blue flame," said her husband. "Yet, who knows? it may also be a true promise that France shall rise in beauty from its ruins."

CHAPTER VII. HOME AGAIN

The next day, they were able to move Father Meraut to his own home. In spite of the excitement and strain, he seemed but little the worse for his experience, and the happiness of being again with his family quite offset the effect of his dangerous journey. Mother Meraut was a famous nurse, and when he was safely installed in a bed in a corner of the room which was their living-room and kitchen in one, she was able to give him her best care. There he lay, following her with his eyes as she made good things for him to eat or carried on the regular activities of her home. Pierre and Pierrette sat beside his bed and talked to him, or, better still, got him to tell them stories of the things that had happened during his brief stay in the Army. Pierre brought the little raveled-out dog, with which he was now on the friendliest terms, to see him, and Madame Coudert also came to call now and then, bringing a cake or some other dainty to the invalid.

If only the Germans had gone from their trenches on the Aisne, they and every one else in Rheims would have been quite comfortable, but alas! this was not to be. The Germans stayed where they were, and each day sent a new rain of shells upon the unfortunate City. The inhabitants grew accustomed to it, as one grows used to thundershowers in April. "Hello! it's beginning to sprinkle," they would say when a shell burst, spattering mud and dirt upon the passers-by. Signs appeared upon the street, "Safe Cellars Here," and when the bombardment began, people would dash for the nearest shelter and wait until the storm was over.

Pierre and Pierrette played out of doors every day, though they did not go far from their home, and had no one but each other to play with. Pierrette made a play-house in one corner of the court. Here in a little box she kept a store of broken dishes, and here she sat long hours with her doll Jacqueline. Sometimes Pierre, having no better occupation, played with her. He even took a gingerly interest in Jacqueline, although he would not for the world have let any of the boys know of such a weakness.

When the shells began to fall, they would leave their corner and run quickly to the cellar. As Father Meraut could not go up or down, his wife stayed in the kitchen beside him. In this way several weary weeks went by. Mother Meraut went no more to the Cathedral. There was nothing there that she could do. The great, beautiful church which had been the very soul of Rheims and the pride of France was now nothing but a ruined shell, its wonderful windows broken, its roof gone, its very walls of stone so burned that they crumbled to pieces at a touch. Even the great bronze bells had been melted in the flames and had fallen in molten drops, like tears of grief, into the wreckage below. All the beautiful treasures, the tapestries, wrought by the hands of queens, and even the sacred banner of Jeanne d'Arc itself, had been destroyed.

Mother Meraut knew, but she did not tell her children, that precious lives had also been lost, and that buried somewhere in the ruins were the bodies of doctors and nurses who had given their own in trying to save the lives of others, and of brave citizens of Rheims who had fallen in an attempt to save the precious relics carefully treasured there. Neither did she tell them that little Jean, the Verger's son, was one of that heroic band. These sorrows she bore in her own breast, but she never passed near the Cathedral after that terrible night.

Sometimes, when a necessary errand took her to that part of the City, she would pause at a distance to look long at the statue of Jeanne d'Arc, standing unharmed in the midst of the destruction about her still lifting her sword to the sky. In all the rain of shells which had fallen upon the City not one had yet touched the statue. Only the tip of the sword had been broken off. It comforted Mother Meraut to see it standing so strangely safe in the midst of such desolation. "It stands," she thought, "even as her pure spirit stood safe amidst the flames of her martyrdom. But I cannot, like her, pray for my enemies while I burn in the fires they have kindled."

There was yet another burden which she carried safely hidden in her heart. She had not heard from her father and mother since the Battle of the Marne. That the Germans had passed through the village where they lived she knew, but what destruction they had wrought she could only guess. It was impossible for her at that time to go to them; so she waited in silence, hoping that some time good news might come. The slow weeks lengthened into months, and at last Father Meraut was strong enough to get about on a crutch like Father Varennes. It was a great day when first he was able to hobble down the steps and out upon the street, leaning on Mother Meraut's arm on one side, and his crutch upon the other, with Pierre and Pierrette marching before him like a guard of honor.

It was now cold weather; winter had set in, and life became more difficult as food grew scarce and there was not enough fuel to heat the houses. School should have begun in October, but school-buildings had not been spared in the bombardment, and it was dangerous to permit children to stay in them. At last, however, a new way was found to cheat the enemy of its prey. Schools were opened in the great champagne cellars of Rheims, and Pierre and Pierrette were among the first scholars enrolled. Every day after that they hastened through the streets before the usual hour of the bombardment, went down into one of the great tunnels cut in chalk, and there, in rooms deep underground, carried on their studies. It was a strange school, but it was safer than their home, even though there was danger in going back and forth in the streets. By spring the children of Rheims had lived so much in cellars that they were as pale as potato-sprouts.

Mother Meraut watched her two with deepening anxiety. Then, one day in the spring, a corner of their own roof was blown off by a shell. No one was hurt, but when a few moments later a second explosion blew a cat through the hole and dropped it into the soup, Mother Meraut's endurance gave way.

It was the last straw! She put the cat out, yowling but unharmed, and silently cleared away the debris. Then, when the bombardment was over, she put on her bonnet and went out. She came back an hour later, to find the Twins sitting, one on each side of their Father, holding his hands, and all three the picture of despair. Mother Meraut stood before them, her eyes flashing, her cheeks burning a deep red, and this is what she said: "I will not live like this another day. Life in Rheims is no longer possible. I will not stay here to be killed by inches. I have made arrangements to get a little row-boat, and to-morrow morning we will take such things as we can carry and leave this place. Whatever may happen to us elsewhere, it cannot be worse than what is happening here, and it may possibly be better."

Her husband and children looked at her in amazement. She did not ask their opinion about the matter, but promptly began the necessary preparations and told them what to do. Clothing was brought to Father Meraut to be packed in compact bundles and tied up with string. Then blankets were made into another bundle; a third held a frying-pan, a coffee-pot, and a kettle, with a few knives, forks, and spoons, while a fourth contained food. The Twins were sent to say good-by to Madame Coudert, and to give her a key to the door, and then all the rest of their household goods were packed away as carefully as time permitted, in the cellar.

Mother Meraut put the Twins to bed early, but she herself remained at work most of the night; yet when morning came and the children woke, she was up and neatly dressed, and had their breakfast ready. She did not linger over their sad departure, nor did she shed a tear as they left the little house which had been their happy home. Instead, she locked the door after them with a snap, put the key in her pocket, and walked down the steps with the grim determination of a soldier going into battle, carrying a big bundle under each arm.

CHAPTER VIII. REFUGEES

The Twins and their Father followed the resolute figure of Mother Meraut down the street, not knowing at all where she was leading them, but with implicit confidence that she knew what she was about. She was carrying the heaviest bundles, and the Twins carried the rest between them, packed in a clothes-basket. On her other arm Pierrette bore her dearly loved Jacqueline. Father Meraut could carry nothing but such small articles as could be put in his pockets, but it was joy enough that he could carry himself, and it was quite wonderful to see how speedily he got over the ground with his crutch.

Not far from their house in the Rue Charly ran the River Vesle, which flows through Rheims, and as the Merauts knew well a man whose business it was to let boats to pleasure parties in summer, the children were not surprised to see their Mother walk down the street toward the little wharf where his boats were kept. He was waiting to receive them, and, drawn up to the water's edge was a red and white row-boat, with the name "The Ark" painted upon her prow. Mother Meraut smiled when she saw the name. "If we only had the animals to go in two by two, we should be just like Noah and his family, shouldn't we?" she said, as she put the bundles in the stern.

In a few moments they were all seated in the boat, with their few belongings carefully balanced, and Jacqueline safely reposing in Pierrette's lap. The boatman pushed them away from the pier. "Au revoir," called Mother Meraut as the boat slid into the stream. "We will come back again when the Germans are gone, and in some way I shall have a chance to send your boat to you, I know. Meanwhile we will take good care of it."

"There will be few pleasure-seekers on the Vesle this summer," answered the boat-man, "and the Ark will be safer with you than rotting at the pier, let alone the chance of its being blown up by a shell. I'm glad you've got her, and glad you are going away from Rheims. It will be easy pulling, for you're going down-stream, and about all you'll have to do is to keep her headed right. Au revoir, and good luck." He stood on the pier looking after them and waving his hat until they were well out in the middle of the stream.

Father Meraut had the oars, and, as his arms had not been injured, he was able to guide the boat without fatigue, and soon the current had carried them through the City and out into the open country which lay beyond. Mother Meraut sat in the prow, looking back toward the Cathedral she had so loved, until the blackened towers were hidden from view by trees along the riverbank. They had started early in order to be well out of Rheims before the daily bombardment should begin.

Spring was already in the air, and as they drifted along they heard the skylarks singing in the fields. The trees were turning green, and there were blossoms on the apple trees. The wild flowers along the riverbank were already humming with bees, and the whole scene seemed so peaceful and quiet after all they had endured in Rheims, that even the shell-holes left in the fields which had been fought over in the autumn and the crosses marking the graves of fallen soldiers did not sadden them.

Mother Meraut sat for a long time silent, then heaved a deep sigh of relief. "I feel like Lot's wife looking back upon Sodom and Gomorrah," she said. Suddenly her eyes filled with tears and she kissed her finger-tips and blew the kiss toward Rheims. "Farewell, my beautiful City!" she cried. "It is not for your sins we must leave you! And some happy day we shall return."

There was a report, and a puff of smoke far away over the City, then the sound of a distant explosion. The daily bombardment had begun!

"Your friends are firing a farewell salute," said Father Meraut.

All the morning they slipped quietly along between greening banks, carried by the current farther and farther down-stream. At noon they drew the boat ashore beneath some willow trees, where they ate their lunch, and then spent an hour in such rest as they had not had for many weary months.

It was then, and not until then, that Father Meraut ventured to ask his wife her plans. "My dear," he said, as he stretched himself out in a sunny spot and put his head in Pierrette's lap, "I have great confidence in you, and will follow you willingly anywhere, but I should really like to know where we are going."

Mother Meraut looked at him in surprise. "Why, haven't I told you?" she said "My mind has been so full of it I can't believe you didn't know that we are going to my father's, if we can get there! You know their village is on a little stream which flows into the Aisne some distance beyond its junction with the Vesle. We could drift down to the place where the two rivers join, and go on from there to the little stream which flows past Fontanelle. Then we could row up-stream to the village."

"It's as plain as day, now you tell it," answered her husband, "and a very good plan, too."

"You see," said Mother Meraut, as she packed away the remains of the lunch, "I haven't heard a word from them all winter. I don't know whether they are dead or alive. I haven't said anything about it, because you were so ill and there were so many other worries, but this plan has been in my mind all the time. What we shall do when we get to Fontanelle I do not know, but we shall be no worse off than other refugees, and at any rate we shall not be under shell-fire every day."

"If we can't find any place to stay there, why can't we go on and on down the river, until we get clear to the sea," said Pierre with enthusiasm.

"It's just like being gypsies, isn't it?" added Pierrette.

"So far as I can see," said Mother Meraut, "we've got to go on and on! Certainly we can't go back."

"No, we can't go back," echoed her husband, with a sigh.

All the pleasant afternoon they drifted peacefully along, and nightfall found them in open country. It began to grow colder as darkness came on. "We shall need all our blankets if we are to sleep in the fields," said Mother Meraut at last. "It's time for supper and bed, anyway. Let's go ashore."

"We'll build a fire on the bank and cook our supper there," said her husband.

"What is there, Mother, that we can cook?"

"There are eggs to fry, and potatoes to roast in the ashes," she answered, "and coffee besides."

"I am as hungry as a wolf," said Pierrette.

"I'm as hungry as two wolves," said Pierre.

They found a landing-place, and the Ark was drawn ashore. Pierre and Pierrette ran at once to gather sticks and leaves. These they brought to their Father, and soon a cheerful fire flamed red against the shadows. Then the smell of coffee floated out upon the evening air, and the sputter of frying eggs gave further promise to their hungry stomachs.

Before they had finished their supper the stars were winking down at them, and over the brow of a distant hill rose a slender crescent moon. Pierrette saw it first. "Oh," she cried, "the new moon! And I saw it over my right shoulder, too! We are sure to have wonderful luck this month."

Pierre shut his eyes. "Which way is it?" he cried. Pierrette turned him carefully about so that he too might see it over his right shoulder, and then, this ceremony completed, they washed the dishes and helped pack the things carefully away in the clothes-basket once more.

They slept that night under the edge of a straw-stack in the meadow near the river, and though they were homeless wanderers without a roof to cover them, they slept well, and awakened next morning to the music of bird-songs instead of to the sound of guns and the whistling of shells.

CHAPTER IX. THE FOREIGN LEGION

Fortunately for our pilgrims the weather remained clear and unusually warm for the season of year, and they were able to continue their journey the following day in comfort. That night they slept in a cowshed, where no cows had been since the Germans passed through so many months before, and on the morning of the third day they reached the large market town which marked the junction of the little river upon which the village of Fontanelle was situated with the Aisne.

Mother Meraut was now upon familiar territory, among the scenes of her childhood. She had often come here with her father when he had brought a load of produce to sell in the town market. Here they disembarked, bought a load of provisions, and once more resumed their journey. Progress from this point on was slower than that of previous days, for now the current was against them. Father and Mother Meraut took turns at the oars, and they had gone some four or five miles up the stream when they came in sight of something quite unfamiliar to Mother Meraut.

Stretching across the level meadows beside the river, as far, as the eye could see, were rows and rows of tents. Companies of soldiers in French uniforms were drilling in an open field. Groups of cavalry horses were herded in an enclosure, and everywhere there were the activities of a great military encampment.

"It's a French training-camp," cried Father Meraut, and he waved his cap on the end of an oar and shouted "Vive la France" at the top of his lungs. Pierre and Pierrette waved and shouted too, and Mother Meraut, caught by the general excitement, snatched up Jacqueline, who had been reposing in the basket, and frantically waved her. Some soldiers answered their signal, and shouted to them.

Father Meraut looked puzzled. "That's not French," he said; "I can't understand what they say. But they have on French uniforms! I wonder what regiment it can be. I'm going to find out."

"We're not far from Fontanelle now," said Mother Meraut; "don't you think we'd better go on?"

"We can't get there without stopping somewhere to eat, anyway," said Father Meraut. "It's already eleven o'clock, and I'd rather find out about the soldiers than eat." So they tied the Ark to a willow tree and went ashore.

In a moment more they were in a city of soldiers, and Father Meraut was making friends with some of the men who were lounging near the cook-house, sniffing the savory smell of soup which issued from it in appetizing gusts. Pierre and Pierrette sniffed too, and even Mother Meraut could not help saying appreciatively, "That cook knows how to make soup." Pierre laid his hand upon his stomach and smacked his lips. "Pierre," said his mother, reprovingly, "where are your manners, child?"

At that moment two soldiers were passing, one a tall, thin man, and one much smaller. They paused and laughed, and the tall man laid his hand on his stomach, too, and smacked his lips.

"Are you hungry, kid?" he said genially to Pierre. Pierre looked blank.

The short man punched the tall man in the ribs. "Don't you see he's French," he said derisively. "Did you think you were back home in Illinois? Why don't you try some of your parley-voo on him? You're not getting on with the language; here's your chance for a real Parisian accent."

"Oh, g'wan," answered the tall man. "Try your own French on him! I guess it won't kill him; he looks strong."

The short man came nearer to Pierre and shouted at him as if he were deaf. "Avvy-voo-doo faim?"

Pierre withdrew a step nearer his mother and Pierrette. "Je ne comprends pas!" he said politely. "Pardon."

The tall man took off his cap and rumpled his hair. "Try it again, Jim," he said, "even if he is scared. They look to me like refugees, and as if a good bowl of soup wouldn't strike their insides amiss, but your French would stampede a herd of buffaloes!"

"Try it yourself, then," said the short man, grinning.

The tall man sat down on a box at the door of the tent and beckoned to Pierre. "I say, kid," he began, "avvy-voo-doo-fam - fam?" He rubbed his stomach in expressive pantomime.

"Mamma," cried poor puzzled Pierre, "he asks me if I have a wife, and rubs his stomach as if he had a stomach-ache. What does he mean?"

Mother Meraut came forward, trying hard not to laugh. "Que voulez-vous, Messieurs?" she said politely.

The tall man was on his feet instantly with his cap in his hand. "You see, ma'am," he began, "we're from the States-des Etats-Unis! We've come here to fight le Boche, savez-vows? combattre le Boche!" He waved his arms frantically and made a motion as if shooting with a gun.

A smile broke over Mother Meraut's face, and she held out both hands. "Les Americains!" she cried joyfully, "des Etats-Unis, dans l'uniforme de la France! Mais maintenant nous exterminons le Boche!" She called Pierrette and Pierre to her side. "These are Americans," she explained in French, "come from the United States of America to fight with us. Shake hands with them."

The Twins obeyed shyly, and when their Father rejoined the family a few moments later, their friendship had progressed to such an extent that Pierre was seated on one side of the tall man and Pierrette on the other, and they were all three studying a French phrase-book. The short man, called Jim, was gesticulating wildly, and talking to Mother Meraut, and she, good soul, looked so wise, and said "Oui" and "Non," and nodded her head so intelligently to encourage him, that he never suspected that she did not understand one word in ten, and cast triumphant glances at the tall man to see if he was observing his success.

At this moment a French Captain came by. The men sprang to their feet, clicked their heels together, and saluted. Father Meraut stiffened into military position and saluted also. The officer returned the salute, then stopped and spoke to him. "You are a soldier of France, I see," he said. "Where did you get your wound?"

"With Joffre, at the Marne, mon Capitaine," answered Father Meraut, proudly. And then he told the Captain of his being brought wounded to the Cathedral in Rheims, of its bombardment and burning, and of his rescue by Pierre and Pierrette.

The Captain turned to the Americans and said to them in English: "We have here three heroes of France instead of one! These children have lived under constant fire since last September, and they rescued their wounded father from the burning Cathedral of Rheims at the risk of their own lives." The Americans saluted Father Meraut, then they saluted Pierre and Pierrette, while Mother Meraut stood by, beaming with pride.

"We will ask them to dine with us as our guests," said the Captain, and, turning to Father Meraut, he spoke again in French. "This is the Foreign Legion," he said. "It is made up of friends of France, brave men of different countries who came voluntarily to fight with us against the Boche. Here they receive special training under French officers before going to the front. These Americans have only just come. They do not know much French, but they wish you to dine with them."

Ah, what a day that was for Pierre and Pierrette! Their story was passed about from one to another, and, instead of being homeless, wandering refugees, they found themselves suddenly treated as distinguished guests, by real soldiers. Pierre swelled with pride, and if he had only been able to speak their language, how glad he would have been to tell the Americans about the return of the French to Rheims, the green poster, Madame Coudert, and many other things! Alas, he could only eat his soup and gaze about him at all the activities that were going on in camp. When at last it was time for them to go, it was with the greatest difficulty that Pierre could be torn away from his new-found friends.

"Come again, old pal," said the tall man, slapping Pierre cordially on the back as he said good-by. "Come again and see your Uncle Sam! Come and bring your family!"

Pierre grinned, although he did not understand a word, shook hands, and ran down the river-bank to join his parents and Pierrette, who were already climbing into the boat.

"Jim" and "Uncle Sam" looked after them as the Ark swung out into the stream. "Au revoir," shouted Pierre, waving his hand. "Vive la France!" And back came the reply like an echo, "You bet your life, vive la France!"

CHAPTER X. FONTANELLE

The shadows were beginning to lengthen across the valley as the Ark rounded a bend in the stream and the little church spire of Fontanelle came into view. "There it is, at last!" cried Mother Meraut. "Thank God, something of the village still stands!" She gazed eagerly into the distance. "And there is the Chateau," she added joyfully, pointing to a large gray stone building half hidden by a fringe of trees. "Oh, surely things are not going to be so bad as I had feared. Hurry! hurry! It seems as though my heart must take wings and fly before my body, now that we are so near!"

Father Meraut bent to the oars. "I will stay with the boat while you and the children go to the village," he said, when, a few moments later, he found a favorable spot to land.

Mother Meraut was out of the boat almost before it was beached, the Twins sprang out after her, and the three started up the road to the village on a run. Groves of trees just bursting into leaf lay between them and the one street of the little town, and it was not until they had passed it that they could tell how much damage had been done. The sight that met their eyes as they entered the village was not reassuring, but, hoping against hope, they ran on to the little house which had been Mother Meraut's childhood home. At the threshold they paused, and the tears which Mother Meraut had resolutely refused to shed when she had said good-by to her own home in Rheims fell freely as she gazed upon the ruins of the home of her parents. The house was empty, the windows were gone, the door was wrenched from its hinges, and the roof was open to the sky. The whole village was in much the same condition. Every house was empty, the street deserted.

Neither Mother Meraut nor the Twins said a word. With heavy hearts they turned from the gaping doorway and started toward the Chateau, which lay half a mile beyond the village. Not a soul did they meet until they arrived at the great gate which marked the entrance to the park, and then they saw that the Chateau too had suffered. It had been partly burned out, but as its walls were standing and one wing looked habitable, their spirits rose a little. At the gate a child was playing. They stopped. "Can you tell me, ma petite," said Mother Meraut, her voice trembling, "whether there is any one here by the name of Jamart?"

"Mais, oui," answered the child, surveying the strangers with curiosity. "Voila!" She pointed a stubby finger toward the Chateau, and there, just disappearing behind a corner of the wall, was the bent figure of an old woman carrying a pail of water.

With a cry of joy, Mother Meraut sprang forward, and Pierre and Pierrette for once in their lives, run as they would, could not keep up with her. She fairly flew over the ground, and when the Twins at last reached her side, the pail of water was spilled on the ground, and the two women were weeping in each other's arms. An old man now came toward them and the children flung themselves upon him. "Grandpere! Grandpere!" they shouted, and then such another embracing as there was!

Grand'mere kissed the Twins, and Grandpere hugged Mother Meraut, and then, because the tears were still running down their cheeks, Grandpere pointed to the overturned pail, and the water flowing in little wiggling streams through the dust. "Come, dear hearts," he cried, "are these your tears? Weep no more, then, lest we have a flood after our fire! This is a time to rejoice! Wipe your eyes, my Antoinette, and tell us how you came here. It is as if the sky had opened to let down three angels and where, then, is Jacques?"

By this time a group of people had gathered about them, the little remnant of the old prosperous village of Fontanelle. "Here are, you see," said Grandpere, "all that are left of us. Every able-bodied young woman was driven away by the Germans to work in their fields, while ours lie idle. Every able-bodied man is in the army. There are only twenty-seven of us left, old women, children, and myself. There you have our history."

Mother Meraut shook each old friend by the hand, looked at all the babies and children, and proudly showed her Twins to them in return, before she said a word about the sorrows they had endured in Rheims, and the desperation which had at last driven them from their home. The people listened without comment. They had all suffered so much that there was no room left in their hearts for new grief, but when she told them of the boat and her lame husband they rejoiced with her that she had the happiness at least of a united family. There was plenty of room in their hearts for joy! "Come with us," they said. "We cannot be poorer. Our cattle are driven away; we have no strong laborers to till our fields, no seeds to plant in them. We live in one wing and the outhouses of the Chateau, but hope is not yet dead, and your hands are strong. Your husband, too, can help, and we shall be at least no worse off for your being here."

Grand'mere spoke. "We live in the cow-stalls of the stable," said she. "It is not so bad; there is still hay in the loft, and there are other stalls not occupied."

Mother Meraut crossed herself. "If the Blessed Mother of Our Lord could live in a stable," she said, "such shelter is surely good enough for us."

Father Meraut, sitting patiently in the boat, was surprise, a little later as he looked anxiously toward the village, to see a crowd of people coming toward him, waving caps and hands in salutation. Before the others ran Pierre and Pierrette, and when they reached him they poured forth a jumble of excited words, from which he was able to gather that Grandpere and Grand'mere were alive and well, and that there was a place for them to stay. He got out of the boat to greet the people, and their willing hands took the bundles and helped hide the Ark in the bushes, and the whole company then started back to the Chateau, Grandpere lingering behind the others to keep pace with the slow progress of Father Meraut.

When Grand'mere, the Twins, and their Mother reached the stable they took their bundles from the hands of their friends, and went in to inspect their new home. The stable had been swept and scrubbed until it was as clean as it could be made. The large box stall served as a bedroom for Grand'mere and Grandpere. Above their bed of hay, covered with old blankets and quilts, was hung a wooden crucifix. This, with two boxes for seats, was all the furniture it contained. A few articles of clothing hung about on nails, and in the open space before the stalls a stove was placed, the pipe running through a pane of glass in a window near by.

When Grandpere and Father Meraut arrived, Mother Meraut met them at the door. "Behold our new apartment!" she said, and she led her husband to one of the clean stalls, where she had already begun to set up housekeeping. The Twins were at that moment in the loft overhead, getting hay for their beds, and Jacqueline, exhausted by her journey, had been put to bed in the manger.

Father Meraut looked about. "This is not bad for the summer," he said, "and who knows what good luck may come to us by fall? Perhaps the Germans will be driven out of France by that time, and surely we shall be able to do some planting even now."

"We have dug up the ground for gardens as best we could with the few tools we have," said Grandpere. "The government would send us seeds, but the roads are very bad, and we have no horses, and supplies are hard to get even though we have money to pay for them. The nearest town where provisions can be obtained lies six miles below, at the mouth of the river, and it is very little one can carry on one's back."

"Is there no way to get help from the soldiers' camp?" asked Father Meraut. "They must get supplies."

"Yes, but they cannot of themselves at this time take care of the civilian population," said Grandpere. "There are many villages in the same condition, and the soldiers' business is to fight for France."

"True," said Father Meraut. Then he exclaimed: "I have it! The Ark! It will indeed be our salvation as it was Father Noah's."

Grandpere looked anxiously at Mother Meraut and touched his forehead. "He is not mad?" he asked.

She laughed. "The name of our boat is the Ark," she explained. "We can use it to go down the river to buy provisions if there are any to be had."

Grand'mere, who had been listening, looked cautiously about, then felt under the straw of her bed and brought out a stocking. "See!" she said. "I have money. The others have money too, but of what use is money when there is nothing to buy and no place to buy it?"

"We must find a place to buy things," said Mother Meraut with decision. "Grandpere and Jacques can take the Ark and go down the river on a voyage of discovery, and bring back the supplies that we most need."

After supper the whole village gathered about the stable door to hear all the news which the Meraut family had brought from the outside world. For months they had not seen a newspaper, and there had been no visitors in Fontanelle. And when Father Meraut had finished telling them all the story of Rheims, of the burning of the Cathedral, of the miraculous safety of the statue of Saint Jeanne, of his own escape, and the final destruction of the roof over their heads, and their flight from the city, the pressing needs of the little village and his and Grandpere's proposed voyage were discussed, and it was very late when at last the people separated and the little village settled down for the night.

CHAPTER XI. A SURPRISE

The next morning the whole village was up early, and plans were perfected for the voyage of Father Meraut and Grandpere. A long list of necessary articles was made out, and the money for their purchase safely hidden away in their inside pockets. They were just about to start down the road to the river, when suddenly a wonderful thing happened. Right through the great gate of the Chateau rumbled a large motor truck with an American flag fluttering from the radiator! It was driven by a strange young woman in a smart gray uniform. Beside her on the driver's seat sat an older woman dressed the same way and carrying in her hand a black medicine-case.

The girl stopped her engine, climbed down to the ground, and approached the astonished people of Fontanelle: "Bon jour," she said, smiling. Then in excellent French she explained her errand. "We are Americans," she said, and at that name every face smiled back at her. "We have come to help you restore your homes. America loves and admires the French people, and since we women cannot fight with you, we wish at least to help in the reconstruction of your beautiful France. Your government has given us permission to start our work here, and has promised help from the soldiers whose camp is near. The money we bring from America will purchase materials, and with your labor and the help of the soldiers we shall soon see what can be done."

For a moment after she had ceased speaking there was silence. The people of Fontanelle were too astonished for words. So much good fortune after all their sorrow left them stunned. It was Pierre who first found his voice. He took off his cap, swung it in the air and shouted, "Vive l'Amerique," at the top of his lungs, and "Vive l'Amerique," chorused the whole village, relieved to be able to vent their feelings in sound.

Mademoiselle laughed. "Vive la France," she answered, and then, turning to the truck, she cried, "Come and see what we have in our little shop on wheels. But first let me introduce to you Dr. Miller. She is an American doctor who has come to take care of any who may be sick."

The Doctor had already climbed down from her high seat and was opening the back of the truck. She smiled and shook hands with the people. "Is there not something here you wish to buy?" she asked. "The prices are plainly marked."

Everybody now crowded about the truck, and in it, oh, wonderful, piled on the floor and hanging from the top and sides, were the very things for which they had been longing so eagerly! There were hoes, and shovels, and rakes, and garden seeds of all kinds. There were bolts of cloth and woolen garments and wooden shoes, and yarn for knitting. There were even knitting-needles! And, best of all, there was food, food such as they had not seen in many weary months. Ah, it was indeed marvelous what that truck contained!

The buying began at once, and never before had any one been able to purchase so much for a franc! Soon there was nothing left in the truck but some bedding and other articles belonging to the Doctor and Mademoiselle, as the people at once began to call her.

"Will you not come with me to my apartment in the stable?" said Mother Meraut cordially to the two women. "You must be tired from your journey."

"We must first see the Commandant at the camp," said the Doctor, "and then we shall be happy if you will find some lunch for us. It is necessary to see at once if our houses have come."

"Your houses!" cried Pierre, so surprised that he quite forgot his manners. "But, Madame, it is not possible that you carry your houses with you like the snails?"

The Doctor laughed. "Not just like the snails," she said; "our houses have been sent on ahead of us in sections, with the army supplies, and are no doubt here in the care of the Commandant."

"Go, my Pierre, conduct them to the camp," said his Mother, "and when you come back," she added, turning to the two women, "I will have ready for you the best that my poor house affords." The Doctor and Mademoiselle thanked Mother Meraut, and then, following Pierre, started down the river road toward the camp a mile or more away.

The next few days seemed to Pierre and Pierrette, and indeed to all the inhabitants of Fontanelle, little less than a series of miracles. In the first place, the Doctor and Mademoiselle had scarcely finished the good lunch which Mother Meraut had waiting for them on their return from camp, when a great truck, loaded with sections of the portable houses, entered the great gate of the Chateau. It was followed by a detachment of soldiers from the Foreign Legion, sent by the Commandant to erect them. The soldiers were also Americans, and Pierre and Pierrette were delighted to find that both "Jim" and "Uncle Sam" were among them. Indeed Uncle Sam was in command of the squad, and when he presented himself and his men to the Doctor and Mademoiselle, he explained that the Commandant had detailed Americans to this duty, as he thought that they would more easily understand what the ladies wished to have done.

The whole place now swarmed with people working as busily as bees in a hive. By night one house was fit to be occupied. The following night two more had been erected, and the soldiers had laid tent floors in all of them. The day after that six more young women in gray came, bringing more supplies. Under the generalship of the Doctor, Mother Meraut was installed in the carriage-house which opened from the stable, and here she prepared meals for her family and for all the new-comers as well. The Doctor established a dispensary in one room of the Chateau, and Mademoiselle opened a store in the basement, keeping there for sale a large quantity of the supplies which had been brought by the six young women. Father Meraut and Grandpere worked hard on the gardens, assisted by Pierre and Pierrette and any other person in the village who was capable of wielding a hoe. Soon people began to come in from the neighboring hamlets, bringing their sick babies to the Doctor for treatment. The great truck was loaded with supplies received through the Army Service and the Red Cross, and the young women took turns in driving the "Shop on Wheels" into other, less favored districts, to start there work similar to that begun at Fontanelle.

Uncle Sam and Jim came so often to the village that they were soon on friendly terms with every one in it. They acted as emissaries between the camp and the village, and if anything was needed which was beyond the power of these determined women to supply, Uncle Sam and Jim seemed always by some miracle to accomplish it. One day the Doctor said to Jim "I wish there were some way of getting a good cow here. These little children cannot get rosy and strong without fresh milk, and they haven't had any since the Germans drove away their cows."

A week later Jim appeared at the Chateau gate leading a cow! There was a card tied to one horn. The Doctor removed it and read, "To Dr. Miller for the little children of Fontanelle."

"It's from the Commandant," said Jim, beaming with pride.

The cow proved such a success, and the babies and young children showed at once such improvement, that the Doctor determined that they should have not only milk but fresh eggs, and Mademoiselle was sent to Paris to make investigations, and, if possible, place an order for more cows and some hens. Upon her return she announced that a load of live-stock from southern France would soon arrive at the nearest railroad station, five miles away.

"It's going to be a regular menagerie," said Mademoiselle, when she told Mother Meraut about it. "There will be two more cows, two pigs, a pair of goats, ten pairs of rabbits, and sixty fowls."

"Mercy upon us!" cried Mother Meraut. "Where in the world can we put them all? Must we move out of our apartment to admit the cows?"

"No," laughed Mademoiselle, "we must find another way to take care of them. The cows can stay out of doors now, and there is grass to feed them and the goats. They can all be tethered by ropes, if necessary, but we must find a secure place to keep the pigs and the rabbits, and the chicken-house must be mended and put in order for the fowls."

"But Madame Corbeille now resides in the chicken-house. What will become of her and her children?" cried Mother Meraut.

"Easy enough," said Mademoiselle; "there is still room in your stable, is there not? For example, there is the granary! It will do excellently for the Corbeilles. Pierre and Pierrette will help build the rabbit-hutch, I know, and there we are, all provided for!"

So it was arranged, and that afternoon another family came to live under the same roof with the Merauts. Grandpere, with his new hammer and some nails, mended the chicken-house, and then helped Pierre and Pierrette build enclosures for the rabbits and pigs out of stones and rubble from the fallen walls.

At last the day came when all the creatures were to arrive, and Mademoiselle arranged that the Twins, Mother Meraut, and four of her own party of young women should go to the railroad station to get them.

The great truck was brought out, ropes were then thrown in, and all the people who composed what Mademoiselle called the "Reception Committee" climbed in and sat on the floor, while Mademoiselle and the Doctor occupied the driver's seat. The soldiers had done some work on the roads, so they were not as bad as they had been earlier in the spring; but they were still bad enough, and the people in the truck were bounced about like kernels of corn in a popper.

"Now," said Mademoiselle, when they arrived at the station, "the fowls and the rabbits will have to go back in the truck. That will be easy, for they came in crates; but the cows, the goats, and the pigs must be either led or driven."

"It sounds simple enough," said the Doctor, "but have any of you ever known any cows or pigs? Do you know how to manage them?"

"I have an acquaintance with cows," said Mother Meraut, "but to goats and pigs I am a stranger."

"Very well," said Mademoiselle, "Mother Meraut shall lead the way with the cows. You, Kathleen and Louise," she said, turning to two of the gray-uniformed girls, "you shall attend the goats. Mary and Martha may tackle the pigs. Pierre and Pierrette will serve excellently as short-stops in case any of our live-stock gets away, and the Doctor and I will bring up the rear."

"It's going to be a regular circus!" said Kathleen. "I feel as if we ought to wear spangles and be led by a band."

"We haven't any clown, though," said Martha.

"I shouldn't wonder," said Mary, "if we'd all look like clowns in this parade."

The car with the creatures in it was standing on a side track, and the station agent, looking doubtfully at the girls, led the way to it, and after the rabbits and fowls had been loaded into the truck, placed a gangplank for the cows to walk down, and opened the door of the car. But nothing happened; the cows obstinately refused to step down the plank.

"Here's a rope," said Mademoiselle, at last, throwing one up to the agent. "I hoped we shouldn't need it, but I guess we do."

The agent fixed the rope to the horns of one of the cows, and threw the other end to Mademoiselle. "Now," said he, "pull gently to begin with."

Mademoiselle, pale but valiant, pulled, quietly at first, then harder. The cow put her head down, braced her feet and backed.

"Come on," cried Mademoiselle to the others, "we'll all have to pull together."

Any one who could get hold of it seized the rope.

"I never played 'pom pom pull away' with a cow before," quavered Louise. "I-I-don't feel sure she knows the rules of the game!"

"She'll soon learn," said Mademoiselle, grimly. "Don't welch. Now, then, one – two – three - pull!"

At the word, they all leaned back and pulled. The cow, yielding suddenly, shot out of the car like a cork out of a champagne bottle, and the girls attached to the rope went down like a row of bricks. The rope flew out of their hands, and the cow went careering down the track with the rope dangling wildly after her, while the other cow, fired by her example, came bawling after. When they found grass by the roadside they became reasonable at once. Mother Meraut then took charge of them, and, as Kathleen remarked, "that ended the first movement." The second began when the goats were unloaded. Mademoiselle took no chances with them. She got the agent to put ropes on them in the first place, and Kathleen and Louise, cautiously advancing to the plank, held up propitiatory offerings of grass.

"That's right," laughed Mademoiselle, "leading citizens with bouquets! Perhaps a speech of welcome might help. They aren't the first old goats to be received that way."

"Hush!" implored Louise. "My knees are knocking together so I can hardly stand up now, and suppose they should butt!"

"In the words of the immortal bard 'butt me no butts,'" murmured Kathleen, as they reached the gang-plank.

The agent, having attached the rope and released the goats from their moorings, stood back and gave them full access to the open door, holding the other end of the rope firmly in his hands. "You can take the ropes when they are safely down the plank," he cried gallantly. "They need a man to handle them."

"Oh, thank you," said Kathleen and Louise with one voice.

The goats accepted the suggestion of the open door at once and galloped down the gang-plank with such reckless speed that the agent lost his footing and came coasting down after them. "Mille tonneurs!" he exclaimed, as he reached the end of the gang-plank and struck a bed of gravel. "Those goats are possessed of the devil!"

The Doctor was beside him in an instant. "I hope you are not injured," she cried. "Is there anything I can do for you? I am a doctor."

"No, Madame," said the agent, bowing politely, as he got himself on his feet again, "I am hurt only in my pride, and you have no medicine for that!"

"Oh," cried Mademoiselle, "how brave it was of you! It's as you say, they need a man to manage them!"

The station agent looked at the goats, who were now grazing peacefully, attended by Kathleen and Louise, and then, a little thoughtfully, at Mademoiselle. "It is indeed better that a man should take these risks," he said, throwing out his chest. "And there are still the pigs! I doubt not they are as full of demons as the Gadarene Swine themselves!"

"What should we do without your help?" said Mademoiselle. "The pigs cannot be roped!"

"No," said the agent sadly, "they cannot." He considered a moment. Then he motioned to Pierre and Pierrette, who were standing with Mary and Martha at a respectful distance. "Come here, all of you," he said, addressing them from the top of the gang-plank; "pigs must be taken by strategy. I am an old soldier. I will engineer an encircling movement. Mademoiselle; will you stand here at the left, and, Madame la Docteur, will you station yourself at my right? The rest of you arrange yourselves in a curved line extending westward from Madame. Then I will release the pigs, and you, watching their movements, will head them off if they start in the wrong direction. Voila! We will now commence."

He went back into the car, and in another moment the pigs, squealing vociferously, thundered down the gang-plank, gave one look at the "encircling movement," and, wheeling about, instantly dashed under the car and out on the other side into an open field. It was not until they had made a complete tour of the village, pursued by the entire personnel of the "encircling movement" that they were at last turned into the Fontanelle road.

"This isn't - the way - this parade - was advertised!" gasped Kathleen, as she struggled with her goat in an effort to take her appointed place in the caravan. "The – cows - were to – go - first!"

"Never mind," answered Louise cheerfully, as she pulled her goat into the road. "A little informality will be overlooked, I'm sure."

Mother Meraut followed them with the cows, and last of all Mademoiselle and the Doctor climbed into the truck and brought up the rear of the procession, with all the roosters crowing at the top of their lungs.

There is not time to tell of all the adventures that befell them on the eventful journey back to Fontanelle. One can merely guess that it must have been full of excitement, since the Reception Committee did not reach the village with their charges until some time after dark. Mother Meraut was worried because she was not home in time to get a hot supper for the tired girls, but when they arrived they found that Grand'mere had stepped into the breach, and had made steaming hot soup for every one. Grandpere and Father Meraut took charge of the live-stock, and Mother Corbeille milked the cows.

As they dragged themselves wearily to bed that night, Kathleen decorated Mademoiselle with a huge cross, cut out of paper, which she pinned upon her nightgown. "For extreme gallantry," she explained, "in leading your forces into action in face of a fierce charge by two goats, and for taking prisoner two rebellious pigs!" Then she saluted ceremoniously and tumbled into bed.

CHAPTER XII. MORNING IN THE MEADOW

As summer came on, life seemed less and less sad to the people of Fontanelle. With the coming of the Americans the outlook had so changed that, although the war was not yet over, they could look forward to the future with some degree of hope. The news brought from Rheims by occasional refugees was always sad. The Germans continued to shell the defenseless city, and the Cathedral sustained more and more injuries, but the beautiful stained-glass windows had been carefully taken down, the broken pieces put together as far as possible, and the whole shipped to safer places in France. The statue of Jeanne d'Arc within the church had also been taken from its niche, while the one before the Cathedral doors still remained unharmed by shot and shell.

It comforted Mother Meraut to think of that valiant figure standing alone amid such desolation. She had other things to comfort her as well. With food and fresh air the roses bloomed again in the cheeks of her children. Soon, too, the gardens began to yield early vegetables. In the morning, instead of hearing the sound of guns, they were awakened by bird-songs, or by the crowing of cocks and the bleating of goats. These were pleasant sounds to the people of Fontanelle, for they brought memories of peaceful and prosperous days, and the promise of more to come.

The rebuilding of the village was begun by the end of June, and the sound of saws and hammers cheered them with the prospect of comfortable homes before cold weather should come again. The work proceeded slowly, for the workers were few, even though their good friend the Commandant gave them all the help he could. There were now a multitude of little chicks running about on what had been the stately lawns of the Chateau, and there were twenty new little rabbits in the rabbit-hutch. As the rabbits could not forage for themselves, it was necessary for others to forage for them, and this work fell to the lot of Pierre and Pierrette.

One summer morning one of the roosters crowed very, very early, and the Twins, having no clock, supposed it was time for them to get up and go for fresh leaves and roots for the rabbits, as they did every day. They rose at once, and the sun was just peering above the eastern horizon as they came out of the stable door. They went to the rabbit-hutch, and the rabbits, seeing them, stood up on their hind legs and wiggled their noses hungrily.

"Rabbits do have awful appetites," said Pierre, a little ruefully, as he looked down at the empty food-box. "Just think what a pile of things we brought them yesterday."

"There's nothing to do but get them more, I suppose," answered Pierrette.

"I know where there's just bushels and bushels of water-cress," said Pierre, "but it's quite a long distance off. You know the brook that flows through the meadow between here and camp? It's just stuffed with it, and rabbits like it better than almost anything."

"Let's go and get some now," said Pierrette. "We can take the clothes-basket and bring back enough to last all day."

Pierre went for the basket, and the two children started down the road which ran beside the meadow toward the camp. It was so early that not another soul in the village was up. Even the rooster had gone to sleep again after his misguided crowing. One pale little star still winked in the morning sky, but the birds were already winging and singing, as the children, carrying the basket between them, set forth upon their quest.

When they reached the brook, they set down the basket, took off their wooden shoes, and, wading into the stream, began gathering great bunches of the cress. They were so busy filling their basket that they did not notice the sun had gone out of sight behind a cloud-bank, and that the air was still with that strange breathless stillness that precedes a storm. It was not until a loud clap of thunder, accompanied by a flash of lightning, suddenly broke the silence, that they knew the storm was upon them. When they looked up, the meadow grasses were bending low before a sudden wind, and the trees were swaying to and fro as if in terror, against the background of an angry sky.

"Wow!" said Pierre. "I guess we're in for it! We can't possibly get home before it breaks."

"Oh," gasped Pierrette, as another peal of thunder shook the air, "I don't want to stay out in it. What shall we do?"

Pierre looked about him. A little distance beyond the brook, toward the camp, there was a straw-stack with a rough straw-thatched shed beside it, half hidden under a group of small trees. Pierre pointed to it. "We'll leave the basket here," he said, "and hide under the straw until the storm is over. Then we can come back again, get it, and go home."

Another clap of thunder, louder still, sent them flying on their way, and they did not speak again until they were under the shelter of the shed. The first big drops fell as they reached it, and then the storm broke in a fury of wind and water. The children cowered against the stack itself as far as possible out of reach of the driving rain.

They had been there but a few moments, when they heard a new sound in addition to the roar of the wind and the patter of the rain upon the leaves. It was the dull tread of heavy footsteps, and they were surprised to see a man running toward the straw-stack, his head bent to shield his face from the rain, under the brim of an old hat. His clothes were rough and unkempt, and altogether his appearance was so forbidding that the children instinctively dived under the straw at the edge of the stack like frightened mice, and burrowed backward until they were completely hidden, though they could still peep out through the loose straw.

The man reached the shed almost before they were out of view, but it was evident that he had not seen them, for he did not glance in their direction. He took off his hat and shook the rain-drops from it. Then he wiped his face and neck with a soiled handkerchief and sat down on the edge of a bench that had once been used for salting cattle. He sat still for a little while, with his feet drawn up on the bench and his hands clasping his knees, the better to escape the rain. Then he began to grow restless. He walked back and forth and peered out into the rain in the direction of the camp. The children were so frightened they could hear their own hearts beat, but they had been in danger so many times, and in so many different ways that they kept their presence of mind, and were able to follow closely his every move. Soon they heard the sound of more footsteps, and suddenly there dashed under the shed a soldier in the uniform of France. It was evident that the first man expected him, for he showed no surprise at his coming, and the two sat down together on the bench and began to talk.

The wind had now subsided a little, and though they spoke in low tones the children could hear every word.

"Whew!" said the soldier as he shook his rain-coat. "Nasty weather."

"All the better for our purposes," answered the other man. "There's less chance of our being seen."

"Not much chance of that, anyway, so early in the morning as this," answered the soldier, looking at his watch. "It's not yet four o'clock!"

"Best not to linger, anyway," said the other man. "That Captain of yours has the eyes of a hawk. I was up at camp the other day selling cigarettes and chocolate, and he eyed me as if he was struck with my beauty."

"I wish you'd keep away from camp," said the soldier, impatiently. "It isn't necessary, and you might run into some one who knew you back in Germany. There are all kinds of people in the Foreign Legion. I tell you, it isn't safe, and besides, I can get all the information we need without it."

"All right, General," responded the other, grinning. "But have you got it? That's the question. I expect that buzzard will be flying around again over this field in a night or so, the moon is 'most full now, and the nights are light, and I've got to be able to signal him just how to find the powder magazine and th e other munitions. Then he can swoop right over there and drop one of his little souvenirs where it will do the most good and fly away home. I advise you to keep away from that section of the camp yourself."

"Here is the map," said the soldier, drawing a paper from his pocket, "and there are also statistics as to the number of men and all I can find out about plans for using them. Take good care of it. It wouldn't be healthy to be found with it on you."

The first man pocketed the paper. "That's all, is it?" he asked.

"All for this time, anyway," answered the soldier.

The man looked at him narrowly.

"Well," said the soldier, "what's the matter? Don't I look like a Frenchman?"

"You'd deceive the devil himself," answered the man with a short laugh. "No one would ever think you were born in Bavaria. Don't forget and stick up the corners of your mustache, though. That might give you away. When do you think you can get over to see that fort?"

"I don't know," answered the soldier sharply, "but I'll meet you here day after to-morrow at the same hour. Auf Wiedersehen," and he was gone.

After his departure, his companion lingered a moment, lit a cigarette, looked up at the sky, and, seeing that the shower was nearly over, strolled off in the opposite direction.

The children, looking after him, saw him come upon their basket near the brook, examine it carefully, and then look about in every direction as if searching for the owners. Seeing no one, he gave it a kick and passed on. They watched him, not daring to move until he turned toward the river and was out of sight. Later they saw a boat come from the shelter of some bushes on the bank, and slip quietly down the stream with the man in it.

When they dared move once more they crawled out from under the straw, and Pierrette said, "Well, what do you think of that?"

"Think!" Pierre said, choking with wrath. "I think he's a miserable dog of a spy! They are both spies! And they are going to try to blow up the whole camp! You come along with me." He seized Pierrette by the hand, and the two flew over the wet meadow toward the distant camp.

"Whatever should we do if we met that soldier?" gasped Pierrette, breathless with running and excitement.

"Look stupid," said Pierre promptly. "He didn't see us, and he'd never dream we had seen him; but, by our blessed Saint Jeanne, this is where I get even with the Germans! Let's find Jim and Uncle Sam."

Reveille was just sounding as they entered the camp and presented themselves at the door of Uncle Sam's tent. During the weeks that had elapsed since their arrival in France, Jim and Uncle Sam had acquired a fair working knowledge of the language, and, though it still remained a queer mixture of French and English, they and the children managed to understand each other very well.

"Bonjour, kids!" cried Uncle Sam in astonishment, when he saw the two children at the tent door. "What on earth are you doing here? Don't you know visitors are not expected in camp at this hour?"

"Sh-sh!" said Pierre, laying his finger on his lips. "Nobody must see us! We have important news!"

Uncle Sam sat up in bed. "Why, I believe you have," he said, looking attentively at their pale faces. "Just wait a minute while I get my clothes on. Here, you - Jim," he added, poking a recumbent figure in the adjoining cot. "Roll out! It's reveille!"

Jim sat up at once and rubbed his eyes, and, after a hurried consultation, the two men turned the two children with their faces to the wall in one corner of the tent, while they made a hasty toilet in the other.

"Now, then, out with it," said Uncle Sam a few moments later. "Que vooly-voo? What's up?"

Jim sat down beside him on the edge of the cot, and the two men listened in amazement to the story the two children had to tell. When they had finished, Uncle Sam wasted no words. "Come with me to the Captain tooty sweet," he said. And Jim added, as he patted the Twins tenderly on the head, "By George, mes enfants, you ought to get the war cross for this day's work."

A few moments more, and the children and Uncle Sam were ushered by an orderly into the presence of the Captain, who was just in the act of shaving. Uncle Sam's message to him had been so imperative that they were admitted at once to his presence, even though his face was covered with lather and he was likely to fill his mouth with soap if he opened it. Uncle Sam saluted, and the Twins, wishing to be as polite as possible, saluted too. The Captain returned the salute, and went on shaving as he listened to their story, grunting now and then emphatically instead of speaking, on account of the soap. When Pierre came to what the soldier had said under the shed, he was so much interested that he cut his chin.

"So that's their program, is it?" he sputtered, soap and all, mopping his chin. "But how on earth did you happen to be in such a place as that at such an hour in the morning?"

Pierre explained about the rabbits and the cress, and Uncle Sam added: "They're from Fontanelle. Their father is a soldier wounded at the Marne, and they lived under fire in Rheims for eight months before coming here. They're some kids, believe me! They know what war is."

"Yes," said the Captain, "I remember them; they came up the river some weeks ago." Then he turned to the children. "Would you know that soldier if you were to see him again?" he asked.

"Oh, yes," said the children.

"Very well," said the Captain, "the men will go to breakfast soon. You stay with Sam and watch them, and if you see that man go by you step on Sam's foot. No one must see you do it. Be sure you don't make a mistake now," he added, "and if you really do unearth the rascal, it's the best day's work you ever did, for yourselves as well as for France. Sam, you report to me afterwards, and be sure you give no occasion for suspicion to any one."

"Yes, sir," said Sam, and saluted. Pierre and Pierrette saluted also.

The Captain returned the salute with ceremony. "You are true soldiers of France," he said to the Twins as they left his tent.

If their comrades were surprised to see Uncle Sam standing with two children by his side while the others passed into the mess tent with cups and plates in hand, no one said anything. It was a little irregular to be sure, but then, Americans were always unexpected! For a long time the men filed by, and still there was no sign of the face they sought. At last, however, Pierre came down solidly on Uncle Sam's right foot, and at the same time Pierrette touched his left with her wooden shoe. There, right in front of them, carrying his plate and cup, and twirling his mustache, was the man they sought!

The Twins stood still, and not by the quiver of an eyelash did they betray any excitement until the man had passed into the tent. Then Uncle Sam said to them, "Now you scoot for home, or your Mother will be worried to death! Tell your Father and Mother all about it, but don't tell another soul at present." The children flew back across the meadow, picked up their basket of cress, and when they reached the Chateau, fed the hungry rabbits. Then they found their Father and Mother and told them their morning's adventures.

CHAPTER XIII. CHILDREN OF THE LEGION

It must not be supposed, because things were more cheerful for the inhabitants of Fontanelle, that they had forgotten the war. They were reminded of it every day, not only by the presence of soldiers, but by the sound of distant guns, and by the visits of German airplanes. Often in the middle of the night an alarm would be given, and the people of the village would spring from their beds and seek refuge in the cellars of the Chateau, that is, all but Kathleen; she obstinately refused to go, even when the Doctor reasoned with her. "Let me die in my bed," she pleaded. "It's better form. Our best people have always done it, and besides when I'm waked suddenly that way I'm apt to be cross." So, when the sound of the buzzing motor was heard in the sky, she simply drew the covers over her head, and stayed where she was, while a strange, half-clad procession, recruited from stables and granary, filed into the Chateau cellar. These raids were likely to occur on bright nights, and as the time of the full moon approached, the people of the village grew more watchful and slept less soundly.

On the night following the adventure of the Twins in the meadow, though the moon shone, no aerial visitor appeared, nor did one come the next night after. Neither did any news from camp come to the village. Pierre and Pierrette longed to tell Mademoiselle and the Doctor their secret, but Uncle Sam had told them to share it with no one but their parents, and they knew obedience was the first requisite of a good soldier; so they said nothing, and nearly burst in consequence. They went no more to the meadow after cress, however. Mother Meraut saw to that. If they had gone there on the morning of the next day but one after their encounter with the spies, they would have had a still more thrilling experience, for at midnight Uncle Sam, Jim, and the Captain had quietly stolen away from camp and hidden themselves in the straw. There they stayed until in the gray of the early dawn they saw a boat come up the river, and the slouching figure of the spy stalk across the meadow to his rendez-vous under the shed. They stayed there until the soldier appeared, and until they had heard with their own ears the plan for signaling the German airplane that night, and for giving information which would en able the aviator to blow up their stores of powder and ammunition. Then, suddenly and swiftly, at a prearranged signal, the three men sprang from the straw, and the astonished spies found themselves surrounded and covered by the muzzles of three guns. They saw at once that resistance was useless, and sullenly obeyed the Captain's order to throw up their hands. They were then marched back to camp, turned over to the proper authorities, and the next morning at sunrise they met the fate of all spies who are caught.

That was not the end of the affair, however, for, knowing that the airplane which the spy had referred to as the "Buzzard" was to be expected that night, and that the German aviator would look for signals from the straw-stack, plans were made for his reception, and this part of the drama was witnessed from the village as well as from the camp. The night was clear, and at about eleven o'clock the whirr of a motor was heard in the distance. The Doctor, who had returned late from a visit to a sick patient in an adjoining village, heard it, and at once gave the alarm. Out of their beds tumbled the sleepy people of Fontanelle, and, wrapping themselves in blankets or any garment they could snatch, they ran out of doors and gazed anxiously into the sky.

Pierre and Pierrette, with their parents and grandparents, were among the first to appear. They saw the black speck sail swiftly from the east, and hover like a bird of ill omen over the meadows. No alarm sounded from the camp, but suddenly from the shadows three French planes shot into the air. Two at once engaged the enemy, while a third cut off his retreat. The battle was soon over. There were sharp reports of guns and blinding flashes of fire as the great machines whirled and manoeuvred in the air, and then the German, finding himself outnumbered and with no way of escape, came to earth and was taken prisoner.

"Three of 'em bagged, by George," exclaimed Jim to Uncle Sam, when the aviator was safely locked up in the guardhouse, "and all due to the pluck and sense of those two kids. If it hadn't been for them, the chances are we'd all have been ready for cold storage by this time. They've saved the camp, that's what they've done! There are explosives enough stored here to have blown every one of us to Kingdom-come!"

"Right you are, Jim," replied Uncle Sam with hearty emphasis, "we surely do owe them something, and that's a cinch. Let's talk with the boys."

That night Uncle Sam and Jim made eloquent use of all the French they knew as they sat about the camp-fire, and told the story of Pierre and Pierrette to their comrades in arms. Not only did they tell of their finding the spies and saving the camp from destruction, but of their Father, wounded at the Marne, of their experience in the Cathedral at Rheims, and of all they had suffered there, and especially of their plucky Mother whose spirit no misfortune could break. And when they had finished the tale, the men gave such a hearty cheer for the whole Meraut family that it was heard in the village a mile away, though no one there had the least idea what the noise was about.

The next day Uncle Sam and Jim appeared in Fontanelle and told the story of the spies to the Doctor and Mademoiselle, and then they held a long private conference with Mother Meraut. The children were on pins and needles to know what they were talking about, and why Mother Meraut looked so happy afterward, but she only shook her head when they begged her to tell them, and said, "Someday you'll find out."

Two days later an orderly rode into the Chateau gate on horseback, and inquired for Pierre and Pierrette Meraut. At the moment he arrived the Twins were feeding the rabbits, but they came running to the gate when their Mother called them, and the orderly handed them an envelope with their names on it in large letters. The Twins were so excited they could hardly wait to know what was inside. They had never before received a letter. Their Mother opened it and read the contents to the astonished children. This was the note:-

"The Commandant and men of the Foreign Legion request the pleasure of the company of Pierre and Pierrette Meraut, and of all the people of Fontanelle at a birthday party to be held at Camp (of course the exact name of the camp has to be left out on account of the Censor) on July 14th at 4 o'clock in the afternoon. R. S. V. P."

The eyes of Pierre and Pierrette almost popped out of their heads with surprise. "Why, Mother," they cried, "that's our birthday! And it's Bastille Day too! Do you suppose it is the birthday of the Commandant also?"

"Maybe," said their Mother, smiling. "Anyway it is the birthday of our dear France."

The orderly smiled, too, and touched his hat. "Is there an answer?" he asked.

"There will be," said Mother Meraut, "but first the others must be told."

The Twins ran with their wonderful letter to the dispensary and told the Doctor. Then they found Mademoiselle, who, with Kathleen's assistance, was putting a new tire on one wheel of the truck. They found Louise mending a chicken-coop, and Mary and Martha sorting supplies in the storeroom. They found all the other people of the village, some in the garden and some working elsewhere, and every single one said they should be delighted to go.

"Now," said Mademoiselle, when they returned to her and reported, "you must write your acceptance."

The Twins looked blank. "Can't we just tell him?" they asked anxiously. "We can't write very well, not well enough to write to the Commandant."

"Oh, but," said Mademoiselle, "I'm sure he will expect a letter, and you must just write the very best you can, and it will be good enough, I'm sure. Get writing-materials, and I will help you."

At her direction Pierre brought paper and ink from her little house, and the two children sat down on the ground beside the truck.

"Now, what shall we say?" asked Pierrette.

"I know," said Pierre; "let's say: 'Thank you for asking us to your party. We are all coming. Amen!' Don't you think that would do?"

Mademoiselle bent over her tire. "Yes," she said, "I think he will like that, but I'd both sign it if I were you."

So the Twins signed it and put it in an envelope and gave it to the orderly, who promptly put it in his pocket, saluted, wheeled his horse, and galloped away toward camp.

The days before the party were full of excitement for the Twins. They thought of nothing else, and how strange it was that Bastille Day and the Commandant's birthday both should be the same as theirs. Mother Meraut bought some cloth, and made Pierrette a new dress, and Pierre a new blouse, to wear on the great occasion, and when the day finally came, the children searched the fields to find flowers for a bouquet for the Commandant; since they had no other birthday gift to offer him.

At three o'clock in the afternoon the whole village was ready to start. Mademoiselle drove the truck with the old people and little children sitting in it on heaps of straw. Kathleen was the driver of the Ford car, and had as passengers Father Meraut, because he was lame, and Grandpere because he was Grandpere, and the Twins because it was their birthday; and everybody else walked.

When they reached the camp, they found Jim and Uncle Sam ready to act as guard of honor to conduct them to the Commandant, who, with the Captain beside him, waited to receive them beside the flagstaff at the reviewing-stand of the parade-ground. It seemed very strange to Pierre and Pierrette that they should walk before their parents, and even before the Doctor and Mademoiselle, but Uncle Sam and Jim arranged the procession, and placed them at its head. So, carrying their bouquet of flowers, they followed obediently where their escort led. "Now, kids," said Uncle Sam in a low voice as they neared the reviewing-stand, "walk right up and mind your manners. Salute and give him the bouquet, and speak your piece."

"We haven't any piece to speak," quavered Pierrette, very much frightened, "except to wish him many happy returns of his birthday."

Uncle Sam's eyes twinkled. "That'll do all right," he said; only of course he said it in French.

The regiment was massed before the reviewing-stand as the little company came forward to meet their host, and when at last Pierre and Pierrette stood before the Commandant, with the beautiful flag of France floating over them, though they had been fearless under shell-fire, their knees knocked together with fright, and it was in a very small voice that they said, together, "Bonjour, Monsieur le Commandant, accept these flowers and our best wishes for many happy returns of your birthday."

The Commandant took the flowers and smiled down at them. "It is not my birthday, my little ones," he said gently, "it is the birthday of our glorious France and of two of her brave soldiers, Pierre and Pierrette Meraut, as well, and the Foreign Legion is here to celebrate it! Come up here beside me." He drew them up beside him on the reviewing-stand and turned their astonished faces toward the regiment.

"Men of the Foreign Legion," he said, "these are the children who discovered two spies, and by reporting them saved our camp from probable destruction." Then, turning again to the children, he said: "By your prompt and intelligent action you have prevented a terrible catastrophe. In recognition of your services the Foreign Legion desires to make you honorary members of the regiment, and France is proud to claim you as her children!" Then he pinned upon their breasts a cockade of blue, white, and red, the colors of France, and kissed them on both cheeks, the regiment meanwhile standing at attention.

When he had finished the little ceremony, the men, responding to a signal from the Captain; burst into a hearty cheer. "Vive Pierre! Vive Pierrette! Vive tous les Meraut," they cried.

For a moment the Twins stood stunned, petrified with astonishment, looking at the cheering men and at the proud upturned faces of their parents and the people of Fontanelle. Then Pierre was suddenly inspired. He waved his hat in salutation to the flag which, floated above them and shouted back to the regiment, "Vive la France!" and Pierrette saluted and kissed her hand. Then the band struck up the Marseillaise, and everybody sang it at the top of his lungs.

It was a wonderful golden time that followed, for when the children had thanked the Commandant, all the people of Fontanelle were invited to sit on the reviewing-stand and watch the regiment go through the regular drill and extra maneuvers in honor of the day, and when that was over, the guests were escorted back to the mess tent, and there they had supper with the men. Moreover, the camp cook had made a magnificent birthday cake, all decorated with little French flags. It was cut with the Captain's own sword, and though there wasn't enough for the whole regiment, every one from Fontanelle had a bite, and Pierre and Pierrette each had a whole piece.

When the beautiful bright day was over and they were back again in Fontanelle, the Twins found that even this was not the end of their joy and good fortune, for Mother Meraut told them that the regiment had put in her care a sum of money to provide for their education. "Children of such courage and good sense must be well equipped to serve their country when they grow up," the Commandant had said, and the men, responding to his appeal, had put their hands in their pockets and brought out a sum sufficient to make such equipment possible.

More than that, Uncle Sam and Jim had two small uniforms made for them, only Pierrette's had a longer skirt to the coat, and on parade days and other great occasions they wore them to the camp, with the blue, white, and red cockades pinned proudly upon their breasts.

Indeed, they became the friends and pets of the whole regiment, and were quite as much at home with the soldiers as with the people of Fontanelle.

Then one day Uncle Sam had a letter from home in which there was wonderful news. It said that the city of Rheims had been "adopted" by the great, rich city of Chicago far away across the seas, and that some happy day when the war should be over and peace come again to the distracted world, Rheims should rise again from its ashes, rebuilt by its American friends.

In this hope the Twins still live and work, performing their duties faithfully each day, like good soldiers, and praying constantly to the Bon Dieu and their adored Saint Jeanne that the blessings which have come to them may yet come also to all their beloved France.

Lucy Fitch Perkins – A Short Biography

One of American literature's almost forgotten names, but in the early 20th Century a wildly popular authoress is Lucy Fitch Perkins, author and illustrator of children's books and originator of the popular Twins series. She was born on 12th July 1865 in Maples, Indiana. Her father, Appleton Howe Fitch, had graduated from Amherst college and spent his professional career working as a teacher and eventually become principle of a school in Chicago. Shortly before his daughter's birth he exchanged teaching for the lumber business and the family relocated to Maples for its forestry. Her mother was Elizabeth Bennett. Both her parents were Puritan, and ensured that a key value in their children's upbringing was education. Though Lucy and her sisters were home-schooled, their parents made sure that they frequently visited Massachusetts and their ancestral home, approximately twenty-five miles out of Boston, where the girls spent time in school so they might experience social interaction with others their age.

Eventually, in 1879, the family permanently removed to the property in Massachusetts, and the girls spent the remainder of their school years here. Lucy displayed early talent in writing and drawing and when she graduated from high school she chose to attend the art school at the Boston Museum of Fine Arts, where she was a student for three years. After graduating, she found employment illustrating for the Prang Educational Company of Boston, where she stayed for a year before moving on to a teaching post at the Pratt Institute, then only recently established.

During these years she made the first inroads into a career in this field, illustrating a translation of The Goose Girl, a German fairy tale made known as Tale no. 89 in the Brothers Grimm's collections, and A Book of Joys: The Story of a New England Summer, which she both wrote and illustrated.

Lucy spent four years working at the Pratt Institute, continuing her own studies while carrying out her teaching duties. She writes of her time there as "happy", enjoying the combination of working on her own talents, while passing them on to others. Then, in 1881, she married a young architect named Dwight Heald Perkins. They had met years earlier while they were both studying in Boston. Their married home was to be in Evanston, Chicago, where Lucy gave birth to Eleanor Ellis and Lawrence Bradford Perkins. They lived here for several years, Lucy working as an illustrator for various publishers and magazines and Dwight as a teacher at the Massachusetts Institute of Technology. They were both active members of their community, and Lucy writes that they "lived fully in the events and thought currents of the time".

She was forty-eight when she was approached by a publisher friend who, aware and impressed by her talents as both an illustrator, which was her profession, and as a writer, which he knew through correspondence, urged her to write. He was so earnest that she thought of an idea for a children's book the next morning, and she immediately set to work making sketches and preparing the idea for presentation. The publisher came to dinner at their house the next evening and she took the opportunity to show him. He responded "go ahead and write it, and I want it". That book was The Dutch Twins, the first in what became a popular series. Using simple language, vivid imagery, stories of adventure and simple moral issues, the stories gently introduced their readers to other countries and cultures, and some of their basic differences with America. Though she had previously published The Goose Girl and A Book of Joys, there is a shift in emphasis from the illustrations to the writing; previously, the illustrations were the primary focus of the books, whereas now, they merely complimented the vividness of her imagery in writing.

Lucy later wrote of the Twins series that they were borne of two key ideas. The first, of "the necessity for mutual respect and understanding between people of different nationalities" if there was ever to be global peace, she felt particularly resonated in her own country, where "all the nations of the earth are represented in the population" (indeed, the term 'melting pot' which we use to describe civilisations where several different cultures are to be found living together was just being coined as a descriptive term in America). The second of these two ideas was that it was possible to hold a child's attention, even when writing about big, complex ideas, so long as the language and story were engaging. As an example, in The Dutch Twins, Lucy touches upon proto-feminist ideas through a childish discussion between her twins about the ships sailing past them as the fish with their grandfather on the dyke near their home.

"I think I'll be a sea captain when I'm big," said Kit.
"So will I,", said Kat.
"Girls can't," said Kit.
But Grandfather shook his head and said: "You can't tell what a girl may be by the time she's four feet and a half high and is called Katrina. There's no telling what girls will do anyway."

This particular interest in Katrina's potential is reflected in Lucy's involvement in several social and artistic reform groups in Chicago, including the Chicago Women's Club and the League of Women Voters.

She saw the need for the themes of each story to be made vivid by their effect on the individuals involved. For Kit and Kat, young siblings growing up together and playing together, witnessing the ships sailing in front of them, the realisation of the female potential is made more vivid than if it were merely being explained to them in a classroom. By witnessing the ships sailing for America, England and elsewhere, Kat sees how the profession of sea-captain is a means for adventure and exploration, and so the injustice of the default, immediate "girls can't" is made painfully apparent. Similarly, to the American children reading the tale, since they can relate to the children's play and childishness, the messages is made more accessible. Lucy writes "I visited a school in Chicago where children of twenty-seven different nationalities were herded in one building, and marveled at what the teachers were able to accomplish. It seemed to me it might help in the fusing process if these children could be interested in the best qualities which they bring to our shores." Over two decades, Lucy wrote 26 stories in the Twins series. The popular children's author Beverly Cleary notes that the Twins series engaged her as an early reader, and ultimately served as inspiration for her writing. Alongside the Twins series, Lucy illustrated Edith Ogden Harrison's fairy tales, which were published in the 1900s.

As she well understood, it remains important to teach children early of the value of other cultures, and the history of one's own. Her writing can still be used as effective learning tools for their playful language, humour clarity still engages a young audience. Moreover, the sketches afford a visual representation of clothing and thereby a subtle hint at costume design for those children so enamoured with the stories that they wish to act them out. The Irish Twins, in particular, addresses "the abuses of absentee landlordism" which partly caused the mass immigration from Ireland to America at the country's birth.

Lucy died while holidaying in Pasadena, California, on 18th March 1937. She was seventy-two. Her books have been translated into several international languages, for their cultural importance is borderless. She writes that she "tried to contribute something to the making of Americans by an appreciation of what has been done in the past to make America what it is today, and of the constructive qualities in the material at hand with which we must build the nation of the future." This altruism and desire for social and cultural awareness and reform survives her, and though America went though almost a century of widespread social oppression, racism and xenophobia, as new writers and activists seek reform, we would do well to reflect on the pertinence and relevance of Perkins's work.